√3 9082 05456631   √ **W9-CBZ-543**

TROUBLE SHOOTER

A HOPALONG CASSIDY NOVEL

BANTAM BOOKS BY LOUIS L'AMOUR
Ask your bookseller for the books you have missed.

NOVELS
Bendigo Shafter
Borden Chantry
Brionne
The Broken Gun
The Burning Hills
The Californios
Callaghen
Catlow
Chancy
The Cherokee Trail
Comstock Lode
Conagher
Crossfire Trail
Dark Canyon
Down the Long Hills
The Empty Land
Fair Blows the Wind
Fallon
The Ferguson Rifle
The First Fast Draw
Flint
Guns of the Timberlands
Hanging Woman Creek
The Haunted Mesa
Heller With a Gun
The High Graders
High Lonesome
Hondo
How the West Was Won
The Iron Marshal
The Key-Lock Man
Kid Rodelo
Kilkenny
Killoe
Kilrone
Kiowa Trail
Last of the Breed
Last Stand at Papago Wells
The Lonesome Gods
The Man Called Noon
The Man From Skibbereen
The Man From the
   Broken Hills

Matagorda
Milo Talon
The Mountain Valley War
North to the Rails
Over on the Dry Side
Passin' Through
The Proving Trail
The Quick and the Dead
Radigan
Reilly's Luck
The Rider of Lost Creek
Rivers West
The Shadow Riders
Shalako
Showdown at Yellow Butte
Silver Canyon
Sitka
Son of a Wanted Man
Taggart
The Tall Stranger
To Tame a Land
Tucker
Under the Sweetwater Rim
Utah Blaine
The Walking Drum
Westward the Tide
Where the Long Grass Blows

SHORT STORY
COLLECTIONS
Bowdrie
Bowdrie's Law
Buckskin Run
Dutchman's Flat
The Hills of Homicide
Law of the Desert Born
Long Ride Home
Lonigan
Night Over the Solomons
The Outlaws of Mesquite
The Rider of the Ruby Hills
Riding for the Brand
The Strong Shall Live
The Trail to Crazy Man

War Party
West From Singapore
Yondering

SACKETT TITLES
Sackett's Land
To the Far Blue Mountains
The Warrior's Path
Jubal Sackett
Ride the River
The Daybreakers
Sackett
Lando
Mojave Crossing
Mustang Man
The Lonely Men
Galloway
Treasure Mountain
Lonely on the Mountain
Ride the Dark Trail
The Sackett Brand
The Sky-Liners

THE HOPALONG
CASSIDY NOVELS
The Riders of High Rock
The Rustlers of West Fork
The Trail to Seven Pines
Trouble Shooter

NONFICTION
Education of a Wandering
   Man
Frontier
The Sackett Companion:
   A Personal Guide to the
   Sackett Novels
A Trail of Memories:
   The Quotations of Louis
   L'Amour, compiled by
   Angelique L'Amour

POETRY
Smoke From This Altar

LOUIS L'AMOUR

TROUBLE

SHOOTER

A HOPALONG CASSIDY NOVEL

BANTAM BOOKS
NEW YORK · TORONTO · LONDON · SYDNEY · AUCKLAND

3400 E. Seyburn Drive
Auburn Hills, MI 48326

TROUBLE SHOOTER
A Bantam Book / May 1994

Previously published as *Hopalong Cassidy and the Trouble Shooter*
by Louis L'Amour (writing as Tex Burns).

Library of Congress Cataloging-in-Publication Data

L'Amour, Louis, 1908–1988
    Trouble shooter : a Hopalong Cassidy novel / by Louis L'Amour.
      p. cm.
    ISBN 0-553-08912-9
    1. Cassidy, Hopalong (Fictitious character)—Fiction. I. Title.
    PS3523.A446T78   1994
    813'.52—dc20   93-37947
                                               CIP

TROUBLE SHOOTER

A HOPALONG CASSIDY NOVEL

CHAPTER 1

MYSTERIOUS AMBUSH

Tote Brown could afford to wait. A man with a Winchester at two hundred yards has all the advantage over a man armed only with a pistol, and Tote intended to give his man plenty of time to get away from his horse and the rifle in its scabbard.

The horse was tied to a willow bush within fifty yards of Tote's concealment, and the rider was working his way farther and farther from the horse. To get his rifle he would have to run toward Tote and right into the muzzle of his Winchester.

Why the man was to be killed Tote neither knew nor cared. But he did not know who had employed him for the job, and that he did not like. He only knew that he had been directed to a secret hiding place where he had found two hundred and fifty dollars and a message made of words cut from a book. The same amount was to come later, if he killed his man.

Tote wiped the tobacco juice from his mouth and settled himself more comfortably into the grass. This was better than the old days when he had been hired to kill rustlers and nesters by the Atley outfit; they had always paid him in the same way, but that had been far from here. The fact that somebody nearby knew him from those days was obvious, but in the past he had received only one hundred dollars per man. Five hundred was more like it.

Of the present case he knew nothing. He had been told the man would be here, near this place, at approximately this time, and if he refused the job he would be letting himself in for trouble. The message from the hollow tree had been very explicit. The words were simple but expressive. *Deal McCarty is still alive.*

One of Tote's last killings had been a McCarty, and Deal was the wily, gunfighting father of the dead man, a very forthright individual who, if he knew where Tote was, would waste no time in killing him. The implication of the note was obvious, and Tote chose to obey orders and take the money.

He rolled his quid in his jaws and spat. The man below was not more than twenty-five, sandy-haired and well dressed for a cowhand. He wore a gun like he knew how to use it, but what he was doing in this lonely valley of the Picket Fork, Tote had no idea.

Obviously the man was searching for something. He had taken a sight on a hill, then walked across to a grove. Now he was studying the valley again, and his puzzled attitude was plain to the watcher. Tote sighted his rifle again, but as yet the stranger was not in the right spot. Moving as he now was, the fellow would soon be crossing a clearing near a lightning-wrecked cottonwood that was somewhat less than two hundred yards away and in the open. If Tote missed, the following shots would be easy, for there would be no cover. Tote Brown did not intend to miss.

Twice the young man knelt and examined the ground. He pulled grass and looked at the roots. Curious, Tote watched with interest. Finally the fellow approached a huge old tree and examined it and the ground around it. Then he paced off an area and looked around again.

What was he looking for? This was not gold country, although it might be buried gold. Possibly something buried here had been found, and the finder did not want this man to know. From his previous inspection of the terrain, Tote was quite sure this man had been here before in the past few days. There were a good many tracks made by this horse and another. That could be the reason. Perhaps the continued search was worrying whoever wanted him killed.

Again and again the man returned to one particular tree. Through his glasses Tote could see the young man muttering to himself, could see his puzzled, worried expression. Suddenly the sandy-haired man pulled his hat down and stared right across the clearing toward Tote!

The Winchester lifted and Brown moved his left elbow forward, setting it firmly in the earth under the rifle barrel. He looked along the barrel at the man striding toward him. It was going to be easy, mighty easy. As the man advanced, the sights moved up his body. When it reached his heart, Tote Brown would fire. As he cuddled his cheek lovingly against the rifle stock, his finger moved to the trigger.

Suddenly fire lashed along his ribs. Involuntarily he jerked aside and his rifle leaped in his hands, fired by the tightening of his grip, a spasmodic, unplanned move that sent the bullet splintering off through the high branches of the cottonwoods, the two reports, his own and that from the mysterious shot fired at him, blending into one.

Lunging to his feet, Tote plunged into the brush, shocked into blind panic and knowing only that he wanted to be somewhere else. He hit his saddle on the run, and the frightened horse took off at breakneck speed with Tote fighting for the off stirrup. Within a mile he had recovered his sense, but his heart still pounded. Hastily he rode into the Picket Fork and began to double and weave like a dizzy rattler to lose any pursuers there might be.

He had been seen. Someone had glimpsed him just as he was about to fire, and had fired first. His ribs burned fiercely, and he could feel the dampness of blood, yet the shock of the bullet was as nothing to the shock of realization that he had been caught in the act of killing. Slowing down, he opened his shirt and stared at the ugly wound. It was wicked in appearance, but the shot had only ripped open the skin along his ribs on the right side.

Tote Brown glanced back over his shoulder. If recognized, he had only two courses: to leave the country or be lynched. The cattle country had no liking for dry-gulchers. He began to take his time, the panic wearing off, trying to lose his trail in the maze of boulders or in the Picket Fork itself.

He did not believe he had been recognized, but it worried him that he did not know who had fired that shot, or who the sandy-haired stranger might be. He would investigate both questions, and when he knew, he would take care of the man who fired that shot. He'd show him! Viciously he jabbed the spurs into the cayuse and started to gallop. He'd show him!

Rig Taylor stared after the man in astonishment. He could not make up his mind whether he had heard one shot or two, but whoever had been lying there in the grass had sure snapped out of it. Walking forward, he looked around. Obviously, from the crushed grass, the man had been lying here for some time, evidently watching his every move. But why?

The sound of a walking horse turned him swiftly, his hand poised above his gun. A tall, well-built man in a rumpled duster sat astride a magnificent white horse facing him. The man's hair showed silver under the brim of his dark hat and his blue eyes were friendly. "Your friend lit out in a hurry," he said. "What was he gunning for you for?"

"I've no idea why anybody would be gunning for me," Rig Taylor said. "I'm not even known around here, and where I came from I've no enemies that matter much."

"Stranger, are you?" The silver-haired man smiled. "Well, so am I. I rode down to look up an old friend of mine. We punched cows together down in Texas."

"Reckon you saved my neck," Taylor admitted. "I'm Rig Taylor, from Kansas. I came out here with my boss to ramrod a ranch for her, but now we can't find the ranch."

"That's something to lose." Hopalong Cassidy shoved his hat back on his head and looked around. "Is that what you were hunting?"

"Look," Taylor said, "this here's the valley of the Picket Fork. The river lies right over yonder. The description Pete Melford sent my boss would put the ranch right where we stand, and the house should set right there where that big old tree stands, but there's no sign of any ranch or sign there ever was one. I reckon the old coot was crazy."

"Maybe I can help look," Cassidy suggested. "My name's Cameron. Tell me about it."

Rig Taylor dug out the makings and rolled a smoke. While he built the cigarette he filled in what there was to tell. His boss was Cindy Blair, and she was Pete Melford's niece. Pete had written to tell her he was leaving his ranch to her, and all the stock that went with it. He wanted her to come out and join him, but the ranch was hers in any event.

Cindy owned a ranch in Kansas, but the range was growing smaller as farmers moved and began to break the land to plow. Pete Melford had unexpectedly died, and after a while Cindy sold out her few remaining possessions and with her foreman she headed west to take over the ranch Melford had left to her.

"We reached Kachina a couple of days ago and started inquirin', but nobody had ever heard of the ranch nor of Melford himself. There was supposed to be a four-room cabin on the place, a barn, corrals, and a good well. But there's no sign of anything of the kind!"

"How long ago was his letter written?"

"About three years ago. He was in 'Frisco, starting for the ranch, he said. But later she got another letter from someone who claimed to be a friend saying that Pete had died. According to them he was thrown from his horse and rolled down a canyon, somewhere near Columbia, California."

Hopalong Cassidy's expression remained the same, but he was doing some fast thinking. Back in the Bar-20 days, he had seen Pete Melford break some bad horses, and he was not a man to be thrown from any horse he would be riding on a long trip. Pete, old as he was, had been a superlative rider, and he made a practice of avoiding horses he did not know. Yet Cassidy's own presence here was also due to a letter from Melford, one that showed a premonition of trouble to come.

The letter had been long delayed in delivery owing to Hopalong's drifting and, after many months, had finally found its way into the hands of Buck Peters, who forwarded it to Cassidy at the 3TL Ranch in Nevada. It seemed to have been mailed shortly after the one Cindy Blair had received, for he had mentioned her letter in the note to Hopalong, and mentioned he was leaving the ranch to her.

What had worried Pete Melford? Why had the writer of the letter to Cindy lied? He had said that Pete had not arrived home but had been killed en route. But Hopalong's letter had been posted from a place called Sipapu after Pete had returned to the ranch.

"Do you know where a place called Sipapu is?" Hopalong asked Taylor.

"Never heard of it."

"We'll ask in Kachina. Let's look around."

Despite a careful search, no sign of a ranch could be found. No fence posts remained, no ash heaps, no ruined walls, no marks of a foundation. Where the log cabin was said to have stood was a tree all of three feet in diameter.

"The old boy must have been crazy," Taylor said reluctantly. "Too bad. Cindy needs the place. She's about broke."

"She sold her other place?"

"Yeah, but there were debts to pay and she gave each of the old hands a bonus. That left her mighty short."

Hopalong moved Topper into the shade of the big tree. If Pete Melford had a cabin, this would have been the site, but this tree was at least forty years old, and there was no indication that anything had ever been built in the vicinity. A well had been mentioned in the letter, but there was no sign of one, nor of the corrals, or sheds.

"Look!" Taylor said suddenly. "We've got visitors!"

Four riders were trotting their horses toward them. All were armed. Drawing up, the nearest of them, a lean-bodied man with an angular, hungry face, looked quickly from Rig Taylor to Hopalong. "Howdy! Huntin' for somethin'?"

"We're looking for the PM outfit," Taylor said. "It was supposed to lay about here."

"PM?" The rider shook his head, his small eyes growing wary. "Never heard of it. No such brand around here or I'd know."

"You never heard of Pete Melford?"

"Can't say I have. Now that's settled, you hombres better slope. We've been missin' cattle, an' folks hereabouts don't take kindly to strangers ridin' their range."

"Can't say that I blame you," Hopalong said, brushing a large fly from Topper's neck. "You own this land?"

The man's face hardened. "That's right! We run it, an' while we ain't huntin' trouble, we can handle any that comes our way, so start movin'!"

Rig Taylor stepped his horse forward. He was facing squarely toward the four, one hand holding the bridle reins, the other resting on his thigh. He looked alert and ready, and Hopalong shot a quick, interested glance toward the sandy-haired young rider. Whatever else Taylor might prove to be, he had nerve. "Maybe," Taylor suggested, "you hombres don't want trouble. Well, neither do we, but we've been shot at and we don't care for it none. We're lookin' for a ranch that's supposed to be right around here, and we expect to keep looking until we find it."

"Not on this land you don't!" The lantern-jawed man kneed his mount forward a step, his hand relaxed and ready. "This is Box T range. Five miles in three directions and twenty miles north she is all Box T, so get off an' stay off!"

"Oh yeah? Well, I have a letter that describes—"

"Taylor . . ." Hopalong cut in. "Give me a chance to ask this gent a couple of questions before we go half-cocked."

For a moment Taylor looked surprised, then he backed off. "Go on, ask away."

"You're ramroddin' the Box T?" Hopalong asked mildly.

"That ain't neither here nor there! Bill Saxx ramrods the T, but I'm segundo. I'm Vin Carter!"

"Who owns the Box T?"

"Colonel Justin Tredway."

"Thanks," Cassidy said dryly. "I'd say that for an outfit that don't want trouble, you're somewhat on the prod. Now, where would a man find this Tredway? On the Box T?"

"When he's not there, you'll find him at the Mansion House in Kachina," Carter said disagreeably, "but you'd do better not to try to run any blazers on him. He's plumb salty!"

Rig Taylor fell in unwillingly beside Hopalong. They rode that way, their backs to the watchers. Taylor was angry and his eyes blazed with resentment. "Don't know's I can blame you," he said, "but I figured you'd back my play."

"Why?" Hopalong turned and smiled at him. "Why walk blind into a shooting match that would get you nowhere? Dead or wounded, you would be of no use to Miss Blair. Didn't it seem obvious enough that it was what they wanted? To me they seemed just a little too much on the prod for honest ranch hands. Where I've been riding, hands swap yarns and tobacco when they meet on the open range, but these hombres had chips on their shoulders."

That was what he had been thinking, and Hopalong's suspicions were aroused by the too-easy irritability of these men. If Pete Melford had said the PM was here, Pete was not wandering in his mind. He had always been a meticulous man when it came to directions, and if his range had been appropriated by the Box T, which seemed possible, then these men were wary of anyone examining the range.

"You think this outfit shot at me?" Rig asked suddenly.

"I doubt it. It could have been them, but more likely it was somebody else. If that bullet had hit you, it could be passed off as an accident. A stray bullet—a hunter who didn't look at what he was shooting, or a dozen reasons."

He reined Topper over to avoid a gully cutting into the range. "Have you been looking around very much?"

"Over a week. I can't believe this setup. The peaks, the rivers, and the town are right. The only thing that's missing is the ranch."

"Maybe that's why they tried to kill you. Maybe they had this place rigged for any casual examination, but when you stayed around, it began to worry them."

"That's logical enough, but who shot at me, that's what I want to know."

Hopalong shook his head. "You've got me. There's either two outfits mixed up in this or one with a mighty shrewd head behind it. I doubt if this bunch of Box T riders knew anything about that shot."

"You may be right." Taylor indicated a tall cottonwood. "One thing is sure—the house never stood there. That tree is all of forty feet and it never grew that high in three years! I sure hate to go back to Cindy an' tell her she ain't got a ranch."

From the site where the ranch was supposed to be to the town of Kachina was all of ten miles, and the two rode it almost in silence, each busy with his own thoughts. For the first five miles the trail led across country through range-land and scattered timber. Finally for a half mile it followed a high-walled canyon. Once on the main trail to town, the going was better, for it was a prairie road from which the rocks had been removed.

"Freighters built this road," Taylor commented. "They told me that in town."

Hopalong drew Topper to a halt and nodded to indicate a narrow, winding trail, long unused, that led back into the brush and up into the hills. "Where does that go?"

"Heard about that," Taylor admitted. "It goes back to an old mining camp beyond Chimney Creek Canyon. No way to get there now as the old freighter's bridge across the canyon is down and nobody's been up there in years. Beyond it there's a big mesa. They call it Babylon Mesa or Babylon Pastures. It's supposed to be haunted."

"Haunted?"

"Yeah. Some sort of religious folk live up there. Folks in Kachina are scared of them. A few years back somebody did start up there—that was when the bridge was still in that led to that mining camp. He found some dead men lying around up there, dead of nobody knows what. Three or four were miners from the camp, and at least one was one of the Brothers from the mesa. He wore a brown robe, like one of them old-time priests. No marks on any of 'em. This feller got out, and right fast."

"And they say it is haunted?"

"Uh-huh. Queer lights seen up there at times . . . That's what they say. I hear the grass used to be mighty good up there."

Hopalong's mind reverted to Pete Melford and his long-overdue letter. Obviously something had warned Pete of impending trouble, and fearing his niece would be left with nothing, he had written to Hopalong for help. But the letter had come too late to help Pete, and there was a big question if it had not come too late to help Cindy Blair. But it might be worth a try.

What evidence did he have that anything was wrong? Pete

himself was the best warranty of that, for Pete had been a practical, unimaginative man. If he said he had a ranch, then he had one. Nobody who knew him would ever doubt that. Furthermore, while such a man might be thrown from a horse, and any man might be, with Pete it was highly improbable. He was the soul of caution. As many horses as he had broken, and bad horses, he had never been hurt. And the horses he himself rode were always carefully trained and gentle.

The facts were, however, that Hopalong knew very well that Pete had survived his return to the ranch. His own letter proved that. It also proved that the author of the letter to Cindy was a liar or else did not know what he was talking about.

"Look," Hopalong suggested, "you go to the Mansion House. Stand around the bar and keep your ears open for any gossip. Listen to anything you hear, for any of it may be important. In the meantime, spot this Colonel Tredway if you can. Don't talk to him, just locate him and see who his friends are. He seems to be the one who has possession of the land; that's as good a place to start as any.

"Meanwhile, I'll do some checking. I've an idea or two that will bear looking into."

Leaving Topper at the livery stable, Hopalong stepped outside and paused there, breathing the cool air of evening and studying the town.

Kachina stood on the edge of a small flat among rolling chaparral-covered hills. The population might have been two hundred people, and most of the buildings were new. Obviously the biggest part of town had only been built in the past few years.

There were older buildings, however, of which the livery stable was one. Behind the stable, which stood on the north side of the street, were the corrals. To the left of the stable was a narrow passage and then a general store, a lawyer's office, the residence of the town's one doctor. Farther on were two other homes, then another store, the Mansion House, and beyond it, the express office.

On the south side of the street opposite the Mansion House was the Elk Horn Saloon, and east of it ran a row of false-fronted buildings, one of which was empty, then the assayer's office, a harness- and shoe-repair shop, the town's blacksmith, the Roundup Saloon, and opposite the livery stable, the Chuck Wagon Restaurant. Behind the Chuck Wagon was a long building of adobe that did duty for a bunkhouse, providing for those travelers who either could not afford the comparative luxury of the Mansion House or who preferred, for reasons of their own, a certain degree of anonymity.

A lean-jawed man with stooped shoulders cared for the horses. When he finished, he came out into the street, lighting a pipe. "Not much of a town," Hopalong said. "Been here long?"

The oldster shook his head. "Ain't nobody been here long. It's a new town . . . grew up around Colonel Tredway's freighting operation. Back in the old days there was a fair strike out past Chimney Creek Canyon, so they built that road and started freightin' to 'em. The mine went bust and so did the town, but by then Tredway was doin' business elsewhere and he started his own town right here. He built the Mansion House and a couple of other buildings." The man gestured about, vaguely. "I come here when she opened up. Folks heard there was gold in the crick down the road about a half mile. A whole flock of us come a-runnin'. There was a mite o' color, but not much. I had me a couple o' horses, so I started rentin' 'em out. There's been a lot of stuff that was freighted in that just passed through to other camps. They made a sight o' money out of that freightin'."

Hopalong glanced at the stable. "This building looks mighty old," he suggested.

The old man nodded. "She was here when the town started. Folks say there was a bunch of outlaws hung out hereabouts. Don't know nothin' about it myself. They was two, three old deserted buildin's aroun' when I come in here."

"Ever hear of a man named Pete Melford? Or the PM Ranch?"

"Melford? No, can't say's I have." The old man pondered the question. "Nobody never lived in Kachina of that name. Leastways nobody who stayed aroun' none."

"How about Sipapu?"

"That's it. . . . The strike I mentioned. Been nearly a ghost town for years. The stage used to stop for mail, but then the bridge got bad and they moved the route."

Hopalong watched the shadows gathering in the lee of the hills and along the east side of the buildings. It was cool and pleasant in the evening in this country, and there was good grass. No wonder Pete had liked it and had settled here. Leave it to such a canny rancher to pick a place like this. Somewhere around the country Pete would have left his sign, for he was a man with habits that stayed with him, and Hopalong Cassidy had known the man too long not to be aware of those habits. Pete had been naturally fastidious. He liked to see things cared for, and he liked things in their place. Also, he was a man who thought of eventualities and prepared for them. Perhaps he had even prepared for this one.

Something else came to Hopalong's mind. "What do you know about Babylon Pastures?" he asked suddenly.

He was unprepared for the reaction. "Don't know nothin' about it!" The old man's voice was suddenly harsh and ugly. "I don't want to know nothin' about it, now or never. That ain't no place for man nor beast, an' you're better askin' no questions about it!"

"Just wondering," Hopalong said casually. "I heard there was good grass up there."

"Good?" The old man looked up at him. "Mebby. There's them as says it used to be good up there. She was long an' tall one time, an' she may be yet, but that country is evil, son. She's downright evil, an' no good can come of trekkin' aroun' up yonder. If you're a good Christian, you'll take an old man's word for it an' stay away!"

Hopalong picked up his war bag and started up the street toward the Mansion House. He had learned a little, although none of it concerned Pete Melford except indirectly. However, there had been no mention of Kachina in Pete's letters and it was possible he had never been known here. He knew how easy it was for a man, especially one set in his habits like Melford, to begin going to one town for supplies and keeping it up, year in, year out.

The Mansion House was a large rectangular building, the lower floor built of stone, the upper of lumber. The wide front faced on the street, half of it given over to the hotel itself and half to the saloon that was under the same management. He went up the four steps to the porch, where several loafers sat waiting. They looked up at him, then away, apparently uninterested.

The lobby was wide and shadowed now. There were several leather chairs and a black leather settee. A couple of good elk heads and one of a grizzly overlooked the room. The desk was high, and behind it was a board with a number of keys dangling from hooks. A register was spread out on the desk.

Hopalong picked up the pen and signed the name Scot Cameron on the line below that of Cindy Blair. Her room number was fourteen and he noted the key was gone, so she was probably in her room.

The clerk was a sallow-faced man with black eyes and a sly, knowing look. The sign on the desk said K. EVENAS, MANAGER. He got up, glanced at the register, then handed Hopalong a key. It was number eighteen. "That'll be two dollars," he said with a smirk. "Cash in advance."

Hopalong Cassidy handed over the two dollars and then asked, "How about grub? Is that place down the street the only place?"

The clerk nodded. "It is, but the food is good. It's quite a sight, noontime. Half the town comes out when they ring the triangle. Big social event of the day."

"Nice place you've got here," Hopalong suggested. "Who owns it?"

"Tredway," the clerk said with a sour expression. "He owns most everything around here."

"Well," Hopalong suggested, "when he landed here, there

must have been land for the taking. A man could do all right then, if he was careful and used his head."

The clerk gave him a sly, sidelong glance. "Or if you were tough enough," he said. "Believe me, it isn't so easy anymore. Tredway owns everything around here that isn't nailed down. I give him credit," he added grudgingly. "He didn't let nothing stop him."

"Some make it that way." Hopalong Cassidy waited, hoping the clerk would continue to talk. "Maybe we'll make ours some-day."

The clerk straightened and his eyes hardened. "I don't know about you," he said, "but I got mine! All I got to do is collect!"

He would say no more, and after a little while Hopalong picked up his war bag and started up the stairs. Glancing back, he saw the clerk was down on his knees in the empty corner behind the desk. Now, what was the man doing there? Had he dropped something?

While he bathed and shaved, Hopalong considered the sit-uation with care. He had learned little, but more and more he was becoming aware that this was Tredway's town. It would pay a man to go easy here.

He had parted company with Rig Taylor on the outskirts of Kachina and they had entered separately. Since then he had seen nothing more of the cowhand.

Pete Melford's ranch had vanished, and apparently into the greater mass of Tredway's holdings. It was imperative to learn just when Tredway had come to Kachina and what he had done here. It also might be interesting to know where he came from.

TROUBLE SHOOTER

That was a question rarely asked in the West, but Hopalong had no intention of asking it. There were other means of finding out.

He was an outsider in Kachina, having little excuse to remain in the area for long; however, if he had a riding job, it might give him a chance to learn a great deal. A riding job with Tredway's own Box T. He grinned at the thought. And why not? He would then be in a position to hear any talk there might be and to ride the Box T range.

At the corner of the hotel farthest from the street, the man known as Colonel Tredway was at that moment opening the door of his suite to his foreman.

Bill Saxx was a big man, brawny and tough. Handsome in a hard, capable way, he was known locally as a gun handler. A gifted leader of men, he was brutal and cunning as well, entirely without mercy or conscience; he was a sharp instrument in the hands of Tredway. Moreover, the two men understood each other, and of those who knew what went on around Kachina, Saxx was the only one who realized the extent to which Tredway was involved or the part he played in it. But even Bill Saxx did not know the beginning of the story or all the motives that inspired or drove Justin Tredway.

"Carter an' some of the boys ran into two hombres over on the Picket Fork today."

Tredway received the information in silence. He had expected it ever since Cindy Blair and Rig Taylor had arrived in town, but two men?

21

"Taylor was one of them. Who was the other?"

"Don't know yet. He was a stranger. Ridin' a white horse. Finest horse he ever saw, accordin' to Carter. Rig was set to make a fight of it, but this other hombre pulled Rig away. Taylor said he'd been shot at by somebody."

"Shot at? He was probably trying to stir up trouble." Tredway's voice was smooth. "Who would shoot at him?"

Saxx scowled. "I was wonderin' that myself. It fair had me worried. I like to know what's goin' on around."

"So do I." Tredway's voice was dry. "Find out who this newcomer is and what he is. I want to know right away. Meanwhile, don't bother Taylor. If he starts anything or gives any of the boys a good excuse, that's different, but I want him to start it. Understand?"

Saxx nodded. "Sure. I'll tell Carter." He hesitated. "Eckerman was over east last night. He seen a light over Brushy Knoll again. I'd sure like to take a pasear up thataway. That there Babylon Pastures always made me wonder."

"Saxx!" The big foreman was shocked at the paleness of Tredway's face. "Stay away from there! Don't you ever go near there! Understand?"

"Sure, boss."

Bill Saxx stopped outside the door and rolled a smoke. Babylon Pastures. What was there about that to scare the old man out of his wits? For he had been frightened, he had been badly frightened, and in all their association Bill Saxx had never seen Tredway get that way about any other subject.

What was there about Babylon Pastures to frighten the man?

CHAPTER 2

HOPALONG MAKES A DEAL

Hopalong Cassidy was out of bed early on the following morning and ate a leisurely breakfast. He saw nothing of Rig Taylor. He indulged himself in casual conversation with various people, and in each case they were soon doing most of the talking and Hopalong was proving himself an excellent listener.

The area around Kachina had been a stopover point for the early wagon trains, but those had ceased during the War Between the States. The freight line had been the beginning of its current rise to importance, that and the mines nearby. Although several minor gold booms and one find of silver ore had failed to produce anything but a couple of low-grade properties that barely paid for themselves and employed a few dozen men, supplying these mines had been the springboard that put Tredway into the shipping business.

The mines to the north and one placer area were served by the town, which was also a supply point for the Box T outfit and a few smaller ranching ventures. Because the town had been mostly created by Tredway's freighting operation, few of the townspeople had been in the area more than three years.

Despite Hopalong's leading remarks, no ranching ventures earlier than the Box T could be located, and nowhere did he hear any mention of Pete Melford. There had to be a lead somewhere. Among the people in the area there had to be somebody who knew of Pete Melford and his PM outfit.

Outside the Mansion House he loitered on the steps, then seated himself. Apparently dozing, he watched the stores open up, watched the various people go to their day's work, and began to get the faces associated with certain places. His eyes were directed to older men more than the younger, and each one he cataloged for future reference.

The whole affair showed every evidence of having been coldly and deliberately planned. Such actions were not too common in the west, and betrayed the mind back of it to a considerable degree.

He was sitting there on the steps when he heard boots behind him and then a voice said, "Tell Vin I want to see him. I'll be in the Elk Horn, an' it's mighty important."

"Sure, boss." The man hesitated. "You seen Eckerman?"

"I've seen him."

"Whatever he saw on Brushy Knoll last night scared the daylights out o' him."

"He's an old woman!" The voice was harsh and intolerant. "Next thing he'll be scared of mice!"

"Mebby, but I ain't wantin' any part o' that Babylon Pastures country myself. Mebby there's nothing there, but where there's so much smoke there must be some fire."

"Forget it, Pres. Nobody is askin' you to go anywhere near there. The fact is, the old man wants us to stay clear away from that neck o' the woods. I think he's a mite scared himself."

"The Colonel? I didn't think he was afraid of the devil his-self!"

"You go look up Vin. Tell him I want to see him."

"All right, Bill. On my way."

Hopalong sat very still and watched the man walk away from them. Pres was a stocky man with decided knee action when he walked; he had dirty blond hair that curled over his shirt collar. He was shabbily dressed, but his gun looked to be in good shape. The holster and belt had been freshly oiled.

He waited for the man behind him to move, but he did not. Cassidy sat there, becoming acutely conscious of being stared at. He let himself start, as if awakening from a doze, and then he got to his feet, yawning. Turning, he saw the big man who stood behind him.

Bill Saxx was well over six feet and his chest swelled the material of his shirt, stretching it taut over powerful pectorals. He was a handsome man, blond, with a wide face and thin lips. He had big hard hands and he wore two guns, his left-hand gun butt to the front, apparently for a right-hand draw. Hopalong Cassidy did not trust to appearances.

Saxx stared at him from frosty gray eyes. "Stranger?" he asked.

"Yeah." Hopalong smiled. "Name of Cameron. What outfit you with?"

Bill Saxx studied him a minute before replying. "Box T," he said finally.

"Need any hands out there?"

Saxx studied him longer. "Might use a good man."

"I rode for Shanghai Pierce, John Slaughter, and the XIT."

"They were good outfits." Saxx studied him. "Know anybody around here?"

"One hombre. Met him outside of town, though, and he seemed to be a stranger, too. Fellow named Rig Taylor."

Saxx started inwardly. Then this was . . . "Oh? So you're the hombre who was trespassin' yesterday? I heard about that."

"Were they your boys?" Hopalong shrugged. "I'd no idea who they were, but I was afraid they were going to jump to conclusions. I was ridin' across country when I heard a horse, then I saw someone all bedded down in the grass ready to shoot a man who was walking below. I took a shot at the ambusher to scare him."

Saxx stared across the street. Then somebody *had* tried to kill Taylor! But who? Why? He shook his head irritably. "You did just right," he said, "but that doesn't mean it pays to butt into things that don't concern you. Ever do any brush poppin'?"

"Sure." Hopalong shoved his hat back on his head. "I grew up in the Big Bend country. You got some riding work?"

"Yeah. Plenty of it, an' some half-wild cattle back in that brush that don't want to come out."

"That's a mean job, but if you want me, I'm your huckleberry." He hesitated. "How about paying me by the head? Turn the whole job over to me?"

Bill Saxx hesitated. That might be the best way out. He had done some work in the chaparral, but the little he had done he'd definitely not liked. It would be easy to lose an eye back there in the brush, charging through it after cattle. And that would get this fellow out of the way, for if he went to work by the head, he would have to rustle hard to make a go of it.

"I can't say," he said. "I'll have to talk to the Colonel." He grinned. His worst headache would be gone. "Stick around, Cameron. I'll talk to Tredway. I think we can get together."

As Saxx walked away Hopalong's mind leaped ahead. No matter where those cattle were, there was every chance of a lot of mixed brands being among them. He might even find a few of the PM steers, for he knew how cattle strayed, and how once back in the brush, they might stay for years if they found grass and water. Moreover, while working cattle in the brush, he could not be seen and it would give him an excellent chance to do some scouting without anyone knowing the difference.

Suddenly an idea came to him. There had been a covered wagon camped on the edge of town as he came in, and there had been a big dog lying there.

He went down the steps into the street and walked swiftly along it to the edge of town. Rounding the corral corner, he went down the embankment to the creek bottom, where a willow-dotted meadow provided plenty of grass. Not far away he saw a Conestoga wagon and several oxen. A washing was hung out on the willows and a cook fire was going.

A big black-and-white shepherd rushed out, barking furiously. Hopalong continued to walk. "Hello there, boy," he said quietly. "You don't want to bark at me. I'm a friend of yours."

The dog eyed him doubtfully, barked again but with less assurance, and then came closer, stretching an inquisitive nose toward Hoppy's hand.

A mild-faced woman was bending over a cook pot and she straightened as he approached. Putting her hand to the small of her back, she nodded to him. "Good morning. Did you want to see my husband?"

A big-shouldered older man came around the wagon and nodded, his eyes appraising. "What can I do for you, stranger?"

"Just visiting," Hopalong said casually, for the man had the look of a canny trader and it would never do to let him know what it was he wanted. "Come from the East?"

"Missouri." The man was repairing a bit of harness. "We stopped in Santa Fe last winter, an' we figger to head north for Oregon."

"I've been in Santa Fe." Hopalong squatted on his heels and looked around the camp. It was no rawhide outfit. The man looked capable and so did his wife, and moreover, their stock, wagon, and household goods showed care and consideration. "Travelin' costs money," he suggested.

There was a flicker of worry on the woman's face. "It sure does," the man replied, "but we'll make her. Although," he added, with a speculative glance at Hopalong Cassidy, "I could use a job about now."

"Is that dog any good with stock? With cattle?"

"Shep?" The man laughed. "Mister, that dog is the best stock dog I ever saw. No exaggeration, either. I used him a lot, an' he's good on sheep, cattle, or horses. But he's worked cattle mostly."

"Want to sell him?" Hopalong suggested tentatively. "I like a good dog."

"No." The man hesitated. "I wouldn't sell him, he's like one of the family. My woman sets a lot of store by Shep. He's company, an' he's a good judge of people."

The man produced a pipe and stoked it. "Mebby you could hire me?" he offered. "You get an extra hand—the dog, too. . . ."

Hopalong considered the question. If Bill Saxx suggested to Tredway that they give the job of rounding up the brush cattle to Hopalong, and the price per head was right, he would hire this man and his dog. Together they could get the cattle out— and Hopalong had once worked with a dog in Texas. A good stock dog could get out three times the cattle that a puncher could, when it came to working brush.

An idea came to Hopalong suddenly. "Ever been in this country before?"

The man's head lifted and his eyes studied Cassidy with care. "No," he said finally, "I never have been here before."

Hopalong didn't press the subject, but something in the man's manner made him wonder. At the same time, Hopalong was impressed with the man. He was straightforward and able looking, and his wife seemed like a woman of character.

He got to his feet. "My name is Cameron," he said, "and I think we're going to make a deal. You stand pat and I'll let you know by tomorrow morning. All right?"

The man nodded. "My name is Pike Towne. You just come let us know. We'll work hard an' steady. I'm not," he added, "a drinkin' man."

As Hopalong walked up the street he saw several people turning in at the restaurant, and he stopped, aware that he was hungry and it was lunchtime. He had been longer in the creek bottom than he realized. Just as he turned to enter he saw Rig

Taylor coming toward him, and walking with Rig was a girl in a divided riding skirt, a flat-crowned hat tied under her chin, and red-gold hair. A few freckles were scattered over her face. Her eyes were hazel and her lips slightly full. She looked trim and neat in her riding clothes.

Rig stopped abruptly when he saw Cassidy. "Miss Blair," he said, "this here's Cameron, the gent who lent me a hand yesterday."

Hopalong thrust out his hand, smiling. "How do you do, ma'am? It's nice meeting a lady. They are mighty scarce here in the West."

She looked at him directly, speculatively. "How do you do? Rig says that you kept him out of a fight the other day—yesterday. Thank you. We can't afford anything like that right now."

Cassidy nodded. "Well, I've had a lot of trouble in my time, but fighting doesn't get a man very far. It's brains that matter in the long run, and believe me, Miss Blair, it will be brains that win for you."

"You don't think Pete Melford was lying to me? Or just imagining things? You think he really had a ranch?"

"I'm sure of it." Hopalong was positive. "But if I were you, I'd not push this too hard for a while. Look around, make friends, and keep your eyes and ears open. You might learn a lot that way.

"For example," he added, "most of the people in town came here after your uncle's death. There could be somebody around here who knows all about him, but they'd be someone who had reason to be in this area before Kachina was built, an old trapper or trader. If we can find someone like that, we can start things."

She nodded seriously. "You've been very helpful."

Hopalong watched them go on into the Chuck Wagon, and then, as he was about to follow them, he stopped. A man was standing by the corner of the building staring at Rig Taylor. He was a lean, stoop-shouldered man carrying an old-fashioned Walker Colt in an open-bottom holster. There was something wolfish about his eyes as he stared at Rig, something that made Hopalong Cassidy's brows draw together momentarily.

Hopalong Cassidy had never met Tote Brown.

Stepping back, he removed his hat and began to beat the dust from his clothing, surreptitiously watching the man. The fellow watched Rig enter the restaurant, then walked on up the street to the Elk Horn Saloon, and entered. He moved with a slight stiffness, as if his side hurt him and he was favoring it. Hopalong went around the corner from which Brown had appeared. A dun horse was tied there, a rangy animal with a Star B brand on the shoulder.

He examined the horse thoughtfully, and then as he was about to turn away, he paused and half drew the rifle from the scabbard. The sight was unusually fine. Replacing it, Hopalong went on up the street and sat down in the shade of an awning where he could watch the Elk Horn.

Suddenly the Elk Horn doors pushed open and Vin Carter stepped out. Almost at once he saw Hopalong, and for a moment he stared at him in a manner that was intended to be intimidating. Deliberately, then, Carter stepped down off the walk and started across the street. That the man had been drinking, Hopalong was immediately aware. Moreover, it was obvious the man was in a belligerent mood.

He stopped directly in front of Hopalong and stared at him, his eyes ugly. "Still playin' wet nurse to that lyin' youngster?" he demanded.

"Taylor? He can take care of himself."

Carter sneered. "He was in over his head. If you hadn't pulled him out, he would have been dead by now."

"Then you should thank me." Hopalong's voice was quiet. "Nobody wants to kill a man unnecessarily. You might be in jail by now."

"Me? In jail?" Carter laughed harshly. "Shows you're a stranger hereabouts, Cameron. Nobody bothers Colonel Tredway nor none of his men. We fork our own broncs up here. You stay off the Box T an' keep that youngster off or you'll both be in trouble!"

"Get out of here."

The voice was low and utterly cold, yet there was a fiber in it that stiffened Hopalong's spine and made him tense with awareness.

"Go," the cold voice continued. "Get back to the T, and if you can't come to town without starting trouble, stay on the ranch! Now get going!"

Vin Carter had taken a step back, suddenly blinking. "Sure! Sure, boss! I'm goin'!" He turned swiftly and started across the street toward his horse.

Hopalong got to his feet. He was facing a man half a head taller than himself, a lean, graceful man whose hair was white and whose mustache was white and carefully waxed, but whose eyes were hard and alive. He was dressed neatly in gray. If he wore a gun, it was not in sight.

"I'm Colonel Justin Tredway," the man said coolly. "I'm sorry my man disturbed you. He's an excellent hand, but under the influence he is apt to become quarrelsome. What, may I ask, is your name?"

"Cameron."

"Ah? The man Saxx was telling me about." The cold eyes appraised him anew. "The man who wanted to get my cattle out of the breaks." He stared at Hopalong again, then looked away. "Tell you what I'll do. Those cattle are scattered over an area better than sixty miles square. The back part of it is desert and rock, miserable country. The nearest part is brush and prickly pear. Forests of mesquite, cactus taller than a man on a horse. Parts of it you couldn't even force a horse through. It's plain hell.

"But there's cattle there, plenty of them. How many, I don't know. Certainly no less than a thousand head. There's some long meadows back inside there. I don't know where they are, nor does anybody, but the Indians knew about them.

"That country is hell to work in. Last year we tried it and had a man gored, a horse killed, and two men injured, so we dropped it for the time being. Saxx says you've worked brush before, in Texas. All right, you get those cattle out of there and I'll give you a dollar a head. Do it any way you've a mind to, but get 'em out.

"You'll find that a dollar a head will pay you well, but I want a finished job. I want those cattle out of there—all of them. Understand?"

Hopalong nodded. At a dollar each it could be a very profitable venture for him, especially with the dog and Pike Towne to help. The first few days would be easiest, and the test as to how much money he would make would be how fast the cleanup could be made. "It's a deal. We'll move out tomorrow."

"We?"

Hopalong nodded. "I've got a man and his wife. They'll cook for me and the man will help some. Now, where does this land lay? Maybe I'm a fool to take it sight unseen."

"Your problem, sir. The brush country starts east and north of here. You can drive right through the Box T and cross it toward the Picket Fork. You'll see a high point of rock—Chimney Butte they call it. Head for that, but when you begin to see a green hilltop, very high and steep-sided but brush-covered, veer toward it. That's Brushy Knoll. You'll cross the Picket Fork at the ford and you're right on the edge of the chaparral."

"How does it lie?"

"Most of the area is between the Picket Fork and Chimney Creek Canyon, but it spreads apart as you go northeast and you'll find a widening V of country back in there. It's not an easy job you're taking, my friend. You'll earn every dime."

Tredway reached in an inside pocket and took out a wallet. "Here is forty dollars. Lay in your supplies and get going. We'll draw up a contract now and my man Saxx will be up from time to time to see how you are making out." He hesitated, lighting a cheroot. "By the way. If you quit before you get out five hundred head, you don't get a dime."

When Tredway had gone, Hopalong considered the matter. He understood the situation perfectly, for once a fair-sized gather had been made, Tredway would see that it was difficult to stay on the job and might even drive off the cattle or force them to leave. Yet actually it was the best chance to find any

PM stock that might be remaining, for if any unaltered brands existed, they would be back in the brush.

Moreover, he had thought of working for the Box T to gather what knowledge he could, but this would be much better than working for forty per month. Not only would he earn better money if he could make the gather, but he would be free to look the country over in the very area where the PM was said to have been located.

Eighty head of cattle per month would pay wages, which meant less than three per day, and once acquainted with the area, they could work fast. The problem would be to keep Tredway from knowing how fast or how successful they were, but Hopalong Cassidy had his own ideas about that.

Pike Towne was coming up from the bottoms when Cassidy saw him. "The deal's on," he told him. "I'll give you forty a month or the privilege of forty percent if we make it. We get a dollar a head."

"Fair enough, and I'll take the forty percent. I'll work harder thataway, an' if we don't make it, you'll be out nothin' but grub." He looked at Cassidy. "You ever worked a pear forest? She's plain hell."

"It is that. But we'll make a good stake and your dog will be all the difference. I said nothing about him to Tredway." Then he explained the deal—no pay for less than five hundred head.

Towne shrugged. "He's no fool. If we try to get that stock an' fail, they'll be wilder than deer. Mostly they will be anyway. An'," he added grimly, "if he could make it unhealthy for us to stay on, he'd have all the cattle we got out at no cost to him."

"Just so we understand."

Pike Towne smiled, crinkling his eyes. "We understand. An' I reckon, Mr. Cameron, this isn't the first time you've come up against a thing like this. I ain't no house dog myself. Between us, we'll teach Colonel Tredway a thing or two."

"But we'll be careful," Hopalong warned.

"We will that," Towne said sincerely. "We most certainly will. Between us, Colonel Tredway is a shifty gent. He didn't get that Box T by saying his prayers reg'lar. You an' me, we've handled guns. Tredway never does, but he has men that handle 'em. Like Bill Saxx."

"I figured on him."

"You'd better," Towne replied quietly, "for Bill Saxx is good. He's good as Wes Hardin, mebby, or—Hopalong Cassidy."

There had been an instant of hesitation there. Why? Hopalong seemed not to notice. If Pike Towne had guessed who he was, it was all right. If he had not guessed, he would learn nothing by fishing.

Between the two of them they bought supplies, and bought carefully. Then they discussed the trail, and Towne returned to the bottoms to load up his wagon and start moving. Hopalong watched him go, liking the man's straightforward manner as well as his easy stride and wide shoulders. Unless he knew nothing of men, Pike Towne was one to ride the river with.

It was shadowed and still inside the Elk Horn. Hopalong stopped at a table and idly shuffled some cards, watching the few men who were around the room. He knew none of them.

Two men at the bar nearby were talking quietly. One was a bearded oldster, a man of nearly sixty with gnarled hands and thick gray hair. The old man wore miner's boots. "Yessir!" he was saying cheerfully. "She was plumb wild around here! Many's the time I've shot deer within fifty yards o' where we stand this minute! Kilt one right out in the street one time. Only then there was only three shacks here, an' they'd been empty for a couple o' years.

"This was hangout for Ben Hardy's gang them days. Ben, he was here for a while an' he he'ped build that livery barn. He was tradin' with Injuns an' robbin' wagon trains. Made a good thing of it. Then he went back to Missouri, an' got throwed in jail.

"Had four, five mighty tough nuts along with him—Black John, a greaser name of Diego, an' a couple of sharp ones. One named Purdy, the other was Fan Harlan. They finally pulled out, it was a long while later that the freight outfit started workin' through here an' they called the place Kachina . . . didn't have no name till then."

Nobody said anything, and Hopalong pushed his hat back on his head and shuffled the cards idly, but with every sense alert. This old man was evidently a prospector just in out of the hills, and if anybody could give him the information he wanted, it was this man.

"Buy you a drink, old-timer," he said.

The old man turned and nodded pleasantly. "Thankee. Don't mind if you do."

"Seems like," Hopalong said as the man crossed to his table, glass in hand, "there aren't many old-timers about. I'm interested in the history around here."

The prospector sat down. "Well then, you've come to the right man, although it's too bad about Dan Crofts. Dan knew all the old ones, even the boys that run with Hardy, an' now he's dead, killed."

"Killed?"

"Yep! Shot down like a dog! Nobody ever did find out who done it."

"Well, I'm sure you have your own stories. You must have known some of the early settlers in this area." Hopalong's suggestion was casual but inviting.

"Knowed 'em? Why, I was prospectin' in here with the first of 'em! I was here afore this feller they call Tredway come. Tredway! I got my own idears about him! I got my own idears!"

"I thought he was the first rancher in here," Hopalong suggested. "He was, wasn't he?"

"Him?" the old man scoffed. "Not by a durned sight! He was freightin' before he was ranchin'! There was three in here before him!

"Jim Turner settled on the lower Picket Fork with a bunch of cattle he brought over from Texas. Jim gave up his ranch an' went back east. Sold out to Tredway."

Hopalong hesitated. "Ever hear of Pete Melford?"

"Melford?" The old man scowled. "I do recall some such name. A Texas man, wasn't he?"

"That's right. Where was his place?"

"It was—" The old man's voice broke off sharply and he was staring at the door as if he had seen a ghost.

Hopalong turned quickly. Colonel Tredway was standing there. His face was graven as from stone, and his eyes were cold with fury. Fury, and something else—was it, could it be fear?

"Peavey!" Tredway's voice was sharp. "I've been wanting to see you. Fellow here last week said he was planning to kill you."

The old man was astonished. "Kill me? Why? I ain't never harmed nobody. Never at all!"

"Come with me," Tredway said. "I'll tell you about it." He glanced over at Hopalong. "You'll excuse us, Cameron?"

The two disappeared out the back door, and Hopalong scowled. Tredway had appeared in a hurry. Had someone told him that Peavey was talking around town? Had he overheard anything of what Peavey had told Hopalong?

Regardless of that, Peavey had known Melford, although apparently the memory was none too clear. Had Tredway come a few minutes later, the old man might have remembered.

Hopalong turned to the door and went out. Before the Mansion House stood Cindy Blair. Automatically his feet turned that way. She saw him coming, and hesitated. "Have you seen Rig?" she asked anxiously. "I haven't seen him in hours, and his horse isn't in the barn."

"No, I haven't. He may be out scouting around to see what he can find."

"That's what I'm afraid of. Rig takes all this so much to heart. He feels that he has failed me, that somebody is deliberately trying to discourage us and get us out of the country, and he worries about my being so nearly broke. I'm afraid he'll do something desperate."

"I doubt it," Cassidy reassured her. "He's mighty sensible, miss." Despite his words, he was worried, remembering Rig's urge to do battle on the previous day. "He hesitated yesterday when I suggested it. I hope he believes he can do more for you by staying out of trouble."

Her lips tightened and her eyes flashed. "Rig wasn't doing any harm!"

"I know what you mean," Hopalong agreed, "but see it from their viewpoint. Some strangers come into the country and start looking over his choicest range with a view toward claiming it as their own. What would you do?"

"It is the best range?"

"It sure is! The PM, if it was there, lay between the Box T and the Picket Fork. That's the best water around here, and there is lots of it. This has been a dry year, but the stream is flowing now with a fair head of water. Frankly, Miss Blair, the sale value of the Box T doesn't amount to anything at all without that range."

He hesitated. "I'm going to work for him."

Her eyes widened, then narrowed suddenly. "For who? For Colonel Tredway?"

"I'm going to get some steers out of the breaks across the Picket Fork. My outfit's moving in there now, and I think before this business is over I may learn a lot more about him than he expects."

She was silent, thinking it over. Could she trust him? After all, what did they know about him? And why should he help?

"Naturally," she said, "you'll do what is necessary for you. Maybe you can help us from there." But there was no hope in her voice, and there was a coolness.

Did she believe he had sold out? Hopalong Cassidy looked at her and shook his head. "Don't get any foolish notions. I've taken this job to help you all right, but I need the money, too, and it's a job I can do. If you come out that way, we'll be camped north of the Picket Fork near the Chimney Butte trail."

They parted, and he walked down to the livery stable to visit Topper. The hostler looked up as he walked through the door. "Some horse you got there, mister. Sure purty."

"Topper's the best," Hopalong agreed. "I've never seen another like him."

"That's what the Colonel said. He was just in here."

"Alone?" Hopalong asked quickly.

"Yeah. He's mostly alone. The Colonel's all right, but he ain't sociable."

What had become of Peavey? Swiftly Hopalong turned and left the stable. A quick look in the door of the Elk Horn proved the old prospector was not there. Nor was he at the Mansion House or the general store.

"Ain't seen him." The swamper at the Mansion House was explicit. "Maybe he went to the Wells, Fargo office. He had a little gold on him."

He had not been seen at the Wells, Fargo office since the previous day.

Worried now, Hopalong wheeled and started back along the street. And then he saw the crowd gathering at the back of the hotel. Dodging around a passing wagon, Hopalong ran down the alleyway between the buildings and stopped.

Peavey lay on his back on the ground, and one glance was enough. He was quite dead.

"Fell," somebody said. "Seen him myself. I was cutting up a log when he came to the window. Had his hands on the sill an' he leaned out a mite too far. Grabbed at the sill, but fell then an' lit right on his head. Must've busted his neck."

Hopalong knelt beside the old man. There was a cut on his head, and Hopalong parted the old man's gray hair so all could see. The blood around the wound was dried.

Nobody said anything except the first speaker. "I don't care. I seen him fall!" he insisted stubbornly.

Hopalong got to his feet, saying nothing. The one man around who could have helped him was dead.

CHAPTER 3

THE PEAR FOREST

When the dawn came, the sky was a crimson glory slashed by the pale darts of cloud, gold-tipped from the rising sun. The mountains were purple still, and in their shadow darkness lay thick upon the land. Hopalong moved out, and beneath him he felt the coil and movement of Topper's powerful muscles as the horse cantered, eager for the trail.

The range lay wide before them and the road was good, for this was the way that led to the Box T. North of the T, the trail was rarely used except at roundup time when the chuck wagons crossed it. From there on to the Picket Fork, his way would be guided by the towering Chimney Butte that marked the canyon that lay on the far side of the pear forest.

Here the range was already dry and parched, there was little grass, and the marks of cattle hooves were all over the land where the browsing animals had sought food in vain. A verse from Isaiah that he remembered from his childhood came now to his mind. *The hay is withered away, the grass faileth, there is no green thing.*

But there was green. He had seen it when he first met Rig Taylor. There was green grass thick along the Picket Fork on the old PM range. Tredway needed that land badly. It would not be surprising if he would steal or kill to keep it. Pete Melford had disappeared and Hopalong was convinced, without knowing how it had been done, that Tredway was responsible for the death of Peavey. A man who falls from a window does not have the blood dried upon his scalp. The old man had been struck sometime before, then pushed from the darkening window within sight of witnesses.

Topper shied at a dark bush and Hopalong slapped him playfully on the neck. "Cut it out, boy. You're not fooling any-body."

The white horse bobbed his head and tugged at the bit. Hopalong's eyes studied the wide range and saw in the distance the roofs of the Box T buildings. By now Pike Towne should be nearing the Picket Fork and well past the Tredway ranch.

More and more his eyes studied the range. It had been badly overgrazed, overgrazed to the point where a little more might ruin it for good. Now the cattle had evidently been moved north toward where the PM Ranch may have once stood, for he saw none at all on this dead or dying grass. Still, the land showed every sign of being overloaded, a condition not too uncommon in the early days of fencing, when cattlemen were still used to the old ways of free range.

Just what was Tredway's financial situation? It might be important to know that. Was he actually getting these cattle out of the brush because he had nothing else worth shipping? It would also be important to know what cattle the man had shipped in the past.

Facing the end of the trail as he rode into the yard at the Box T was the ranch house, a long, low building with a wide veranda fronting it. To the right was the bunkhouse and to the left the stables, toolshed, and blacksmith shop. Behind the barn but in sight were the horse corrals.

The only man in sight sat smoking on the steps of the bunkhouse. As the sound of the horse's hooves came to him, he turned sharply, then got to his feet as he recognized Hopalong. He spoke sharply over his shoulder and moved slightly out of the way as Vin Carter showed in the doorway.

Carter stared for a minute and then walked down the steps. "You huntin' trouble?" he demanded. "I told you to stay off this place!"

"Your boss thinks different," Hopalong replied calmly. "I'm working on this spread."

Carter's eyes glinted. "Well then, that puts you under my orders!"

Hopalong smiled cheerfully, shoving his hat back from the faded white scar on his brow. Mildly amused, he looked at Carter. There was innate viciousness in the man, and if he avoided trouble with him, he would be fortunate. "Sorry, Carter, I'm under nobody's orders. I'm contracting. I'm getting cattle out of the pear forest for Tredway."

Carter stared, then he laughed. "Why, you fool! Nobody can get them cows out of there! You ever tried to use a rope in brush so thick you can barely push a way through the thinnest parts?

You ever tackled a sixteen-hundred-pound longhorn at close quarters? How many men you usin'?"

"One," Hopalong said, "besides myself. We'll handle it."

Carter snorted and spat. "Why, I was aimin' to take your scalp, but I'd be a fool to waste lead on a tinhorn that would tackle a job like that! You won't last a week!" He laughed. "Go to it. If you get a hundred head out of there, I'll eat my shirt an' yours, too!"

Hopalong chuckled. "I've got to get out more than that. I've got to get five hundred head out or no deal."

Vin Carter's eyes glinted. "Yeah? This I gotta see!"

"You will!" Hopalong was cheerful. He turned Topper to the north and followed out, riding along the tracks of the broad-tired wagon. Dust arose at each step the horse took. The Box T range was in bad shape. Very bad.

From Carter's attitude it was obvious that the Box T hands wanted no part of the forest of prickly pear and mesquite, and knowing such country, he could not find it in his heart to blame them. It was hell to work, and nobody knew that better than he.

The sun was high, and he mopped his brow and rode on, the salt of the sweat smarting his eyes. The sun reflected from the barren range as from a desert or salt bed. The mountains were close now, and the towering finger of Chimney Butte was plain to see. Soon he should be sighting Brushy Knoll. His eyes swung eastward then, toward the strange, high mesa that was Babylon Pastures. The mystery of the place intrigued him. The bridge was down, they had said, on the trail that led that way, and that trail was miles away to the east, but suppose there was another way? A route that led to the vicinity of Brushy Knoll, where strange lights had been seen? What was it that was up there on the mesa to frighten a man like Tredway? What was up there that was strange?

The landscape began a change that was only subtle at first, for the grass grew gray and then turned to pale green. They were nearing the Picket Fork now, although it was still miles away. Already, however, its effects were being felt. A coyote appeared, then vanished into an arroyo. The land grew more rolling, and the shallow valleys were greener and the grass grew taller. Now, for the first time, he began to see cattle, but they were painfully few.

There might be more than one way for Cindy Blair to regain her ranch; Colonel Tredway might not be so secure as was generally imagined. He pushed on, and it was well past noon before he sighted the Picket Fork. He drew up on a long ridge, and standing in his stirrups, he searched the banks of the stream.

After a moment his eyes caught a faint trail of smoke, and he swung the white horse toward it. Pike Towne was on his feet to welcome him when Hopalong rode into camp. His wife turned and smiled at Hopalong.

"Glad to see you, Cameron!" Towne said. "I was afraid you might have had trouble in town."

"No trouble," Hopalong said, "but I'll have it with Vin Carter one of these days."

Towne nodded seriously. "Yeah, he's a cantankerous cuss. Somethin' eatin' on him all the time." He handed Hoppy a plate. "There's somebody else around here it would pay to keep your eyes on. I spotted him in town the other day. His name is Tote Brown. Thin, stoop-shouldered hombre, never clean-shaved, an' always packin' a rifle. He's a back shooter.

"Up north," he added, "some cattlemen hired him to clean out nesters an' rustlers at so much a head. Nobody knows how many he got. I doubt if anybody around here knows him or even knows about him. He ain't talkative, an' he had to get out of that country before they hung him, so he ain't exactly anxious to have folks know who he is."

Hopalong had stopped, listening intently, his mind back with the mysterious marksman who had taken a shot at Rig Taylor. His own shot had spoiled the man's aim, and perhaps scratched him, but he had a mere glimpse of the killer. Yet this might be the man, and it was such a man who had left the dun horse hitched around the corner of the Chuck Wagon Restaurant, and his Winchester had been fixed with an especially fine sight. "I think I've seen him," Hopalong said. "Thanks for the tip."

Towne nodded, speared a chunk of beef, and began to ladle beans to his plate. "This here," he added seriously, "is no country for a pilgrim. A man who expects to stay alive had better keep his eyes open. There's plenty of folks around here with secrets they want to keep, an' if they get an idea somebody is too curious, they'll shoot, an' shoot quick."

"Looked this country over yet?" Hopalong jerked his head toward the land beyond the Picket Fork.

"Thought I'd wait for you. There was plenty to do, anyway. I had to cut a stock of wood for Sarah and rustle up some rocks for a fireplace. From here, though, she looks mighty mean."

The beans were excellent and the steak was broiled just as he liked it, thick and juicy. He ate more than he had planned, listening to the talk between Pike Towne and his wife. That there was a strong bond of affection between them was obvious.

Shep had come up to Hopalong, and after sniffing inquisitively of his sleeve, he lay down beside him and rested his nose on his paws. Pike glanced at him and smiled. "Reckon Shep figures you are all right," he said. "He's mighty touchy about strangers as a rule."

"This afternoon," Hopalong said, "we'll scout a little. You go one way, I'll take another. Make an estimate of the cattle you see, but mostly I want to find a large open space well back into the pear forest. I want a place that's hard to find, with good grass, and water if possible."

Towne looked at him curiously. "Yeah," he said. "I think we can find a place like that. I hear there's clearings back in there that are hundreds of acres in extent. After we find it, what then?"

"We'll build a good-sized corral out here," Hopalong said, "but we'll also make a fair corral back in that clearing, mostly by working the limbs of the mesquite together. Probably we can find a place that will need only a little work to keep it safe so the cattle won't stray."

Towne chuckled. "I get it. You're figurin' to keep most of the cattle back inside so nobody will know how many you're gettin' out. Is that it?"

Cassidy nodded. "It seems to me," he said, "that a certain

hombre might let us get out, say, four hundred head or better. Then someone might run them off before we could begin to collect. I don't figure to let anybody know how we're fixed."

"Good idea." Towne started to speak, then said nothing further, but when he got up and wiped his hands on a handful of grass, he said, "I'll head off toward Chimney Butte. I figure that might be a good place to look."

"Go ahead," Hoppy said. "I'll work farther east."

Hopalong got to his feet and glanced at Sarah Towne. "Thanks," he said, smiling. "That was the best meal I've eaten in a long time. Pike sure found a good cook when he found you."

She flushed with pleasure. "Pike likes good food," she said. "He's a big eater, and I like that. It's no pleasure to cook for a man who picks over his food. He's like you—he never leaves anything on his plate."

Hopalong saddled Topper again and, putting the bit between his teeth, slipped the bridle over his ears. "It's a long time since you've been in the brush, Topper," he said, "but you'll get a taste of it today."

He went down the bank and waded the horse through the ten-foot-wide Picket Fork and up the opposite bank. The trees were thick, but he rode through them and found himself facing an impenetrable wall of brush. As he skirted it, searching for an opening, he studied the varieties he saw. Before him were thousands of acres of black chaparral, dense thickets of mingled mesquite, towering prickly pear, low-growing catclaw with its dangerous thorns that hook into the hooves of cattle or horses, and colima with its spines. Everything here had a thorn, long and dangerous, some of them poisonous, all of them needle-pointed. Once within these close confines, there were no land-marks, nothing but a man's own trail to guide him.

Walls of jonco brush, all spines and ugly as sin, devil's head, and yucca; it was all here in a dense tangle. And under it moved a myriad of life-forms: rattlesnakes, javelinas, and many varieties of birds and lizards. It was a morass without water, a maze with-out plan, a trap that could grip and hold a man for days. Once lost, only chance could help a man escape. Even when fairly cool where there was a breeze, within the black chaparral the air was close and sweat streamed down your body, soaking your cloth-ing. Thorns snagged at the clothes and skin. You jerked free from one thorn to be stabbed by another. Only heavy leather, hot as Hades, offered protection. This was exactly like the dreaded monte of Mexico and Texas.

Hopalong rode slowly along that thorny rampart, alert for any opening that might allow him to enter. Twice he believed he had found what he wanted, but each time it proved to be only a deviation in the wall of brush, and there was no entry.

As he skirted the chaparral he thought of the problem that faced him. The wild cattle of the brush country had lost all do-mestication. They lived for the wilderness, and he had known of cases where, when removed from the brush, the cattle simply lay down and died, refusing to be driven despite torture and beating. And they were utterly savage, fighting anything that came into their path, possessed of the speed of a deer and the agility of a panther. He who has not encountered wild cattle in their native habitat can have no idea of their nature.

Now the wall bellied out before him, and swinging wide to skirt it, Hopalong suddenly saw a projecting corner of rock. Riding nearer, he found that a huge fault in the surface had thrust a rocky ledge from the earth on a steep incline. Beneath its shade the brush had not gathered, and it seemed to offer entry to the wall of brush. Topper went forward, his ears pricked with curiosity, and avoiding with dainty steps the reaching spines of the catclaw. Rounding the corner of the ledge, Hopalong saw a narrow avenue before him and he saw cow tracks, some of them amazingly large, along the earth and sand that formed the trail.

Carefully he pushed on, and the close, deadly air of the chaparral settled about him, confining and sticky with heat. Sweat trickled down the back of his neck and under his arms. Dust arose from beneath him and settled over his clothing. The reaching spines of the pear snagged at his clothing, only sliding off the stiff leather of his chaps.

Yet the trail continued. Once he had seen those tracks, Hopalong knew that he had found an entry to that backcountry of the bush. Somewhere far ahead he heard a steer lowing. It was a soft, distant, moaning sound. He moved steadily on, the walls of the chaparral so close that a lifted hand would be snagged by the spines. Overhead was a single strip of brassy sky. He halted, talking softly to Topper, and let the horse breathe a little, yet it was almost better to be moving. Once they entered a small clearing, about half an acre in area. Here they paused longer. There were cow tracks all about now, and here and there smaller alleyways led off into the brush waste.

Chimney Butte might as well have been a thousand miles away, for from here it could not be seen. He spotted a big steer, its huge horns all of five feet across. It lifted its head and stared at him, but made no move to attack, merely snuffing suspiciously at the scent of horse and man.

It was well nigh impossible to estimate distance in the chaparral. The trail twisted and turned, and occasionally he had to double back and try again. Usually the tracks helped, but the rock wall of the upthrust had long since fallen behind. Then he began to encounter more and more clearings, small but grassy, and in many of them the grass was remarkably green. Because of the roots, very little rain that fell on this land ever ran off. Yet these clearings would grow fewer and fewer as time went on, and eventually there would be none at all. The brush would have covered every available foot of it. This brush was a thorny-handed monster, an octopus of the plains and desert country, never satiated while anything remained to be taken and to be bound in the clinging tentacles of its roots.

Suddenly Hopalong rode out into a huge clearing that must have been all of half a mile long and more than a quarter of a mile wide. Here at least thirty head of cattle were feeding or lying about on the grass. They got up and stared at him, and one bull came toward them, lowing deep in his chest and kicking dust over his back, his big head lowered, his eyes rolling. That bull, Hopalong reflected, must weigh all of twenty-two hundred and his head and sides were scarred by many battles.

Hopalong swung wide around him and, mopping sweat from his face, searched the opposite wall for a way out of the clearing. He found it, and then continued to search until he had located more cattle and more clearings. It was late afternoon before he started back. He had seen at least a hundred head of cattle, and heard many more, and he doubted if he had more than touched the huge mass of the chaparral.

It was dark when he reached camp, and he rode toward the firelight, hot and weary. Pike was already in, seated on a fallen log with a tin cup of coffee. He grinned at Hopalong. "Got into it, I see. Find much?"

When Cassidy had told him of his day's venture into the brush, Pike nodded. "I reckon I saw about as many as you did. There's plenty of cattle in there, all right, and from the way they act, they haven't been bothered much. Notice any brands other than Box T?"

"No, not a one," Hopalong admitted, "but most of this stock has never been branded. How about you?"

"Same as you. No other brands." He hesitated, then reaching for the coffeepot, he said casually, "Found a place to hold our cows. Old corral back in there. The fence is all overgrown, but she was built tight. Now the brush has grown all through the posts and rails so it's that much tighter. It's big—big enough to hold a thousand head if necessary. I reckon somebody threw it up some years back. It was built about like you suggested, just pieced together wherever the brush wasn't tight enough to hold 'em."

"Water?"

"Yeah. Looks like she might be an old rustlers hangout."

Hopalong nodded. "I imagine," he said carefully, not looking at Pike Towne, "that they have been in this country. We'll have to try to find if they had a way out on the other side."

Towne's face stiffened queerly. He shot a sharp glance at Hopalong and set his cup down on a rock. "You wasn't figurin' on rustlin', were you?"

Hopalong was mildly surprised. "No. Why?"

"Nothin'. I didn't figure you would, but anyway, I want no part in anything that isn't legal."

"My feelings, too," Hopalong assured him, "but a way out might be convenient."

"There's an old trail," Pike said thoughtfully, "east of here. You must have seen it. The trail leaves the road to the Box T about ten miles out of Kachina, heads northeast. That trail must pass close to the bend of the Picket Fork. We might find a way out that way."

"We might," Hopalong agreed.

He was growing more and more curious about Pike Towne, and he had been almost positive that Towne, if left alone, would find the kind of clearing they sought. If the big man had not at one time lived in the area, Hopalong Cassidy would be badly fooled. Whether he had been an outlaw himself, Hopalong had no idea. What he did know was that Pike was concealing something, but in his own good time he might talk.

Somewhere a coyote yapped shrilly into the night, and a nighthawk swooped close, then winged on away into the darkness. Stars came out, thick and bright, seeming so close about them that it appeared a man might reach up and knock them down with a stick.

He ate in silence, and again Shep came to lie beside him. Pike lit his pipe, and they dozed. And then, suddenly, it came!

Hopalong stiffened, almost dropping his cup. Pike Towne's face blanched and his wife stared at him, her cheeks drawn and pale.

High and clear, sounding distant, yet close, there came the sound of voices on the wind. A long, hollow call. A pause, then an answering chorus. The sound faded, then swept back; although distorted as it was by the distance, they could hear the unmistakable rhythm of words and phrases.

The weird chanting reached out into the night and then ended. A strange cry filled with loneliness and memories of terror, a cry that chilled their spines and left the three staring, the echo of it hanging in their ears.

"What was that?" Hopalong demanded, of nobody in particular.

There was no answer, for there was none to be given. Then it came again, and again it sounded long and clear and somehow unearthly. It might have come from the range behind them. It might have come from up- or down-stream, or from the wastes of the chaparral, but they all knew it did not. It came from farther away, maybe miles away.

Nobody said anything for several minutes, and then Hopalong glanced over at Pike. The man's face was haunted by memory, and when he turned, his lips started to form words, then stopped. The fire crackled and a stick fell, then sparks sprang up, following the trail of the smoke. After a minute a coyote lifted his plaintive voice high into a shrill yelping that chattered off down a long hill of sound, then died away.

"Now that was quite a sound," Hoppy said. "Ever hear it before, Pike?"

Towne's lips were tight, his eyes cold. A moment passed before he replied, and it was with a question. "Why ask me? What makes you think I might have?"

"A hunch."

Pike studied Cassidy while Sarah Towne's eyes went from one to the other, half-frightened, half-hopeful. It was the hopefulness that made Hopalong curious. Topper stamped in the tall grass and blew contentedly. Firelight flickered on his flanks and glistened on the shining coats of the darker horses.

"What you lookin' for?" Pike's voice promised nothing.

"I want to know who killed Pete Melford."

"I don't know anything about that. I've got my own questions to look into hereabouts." Pike's lids flickered ever so slightly. "We may be out here doin' the same kinda thing, Cameron. But we ain't doin' it for the same reasons."

Hopalong examined Pike Towne narrowly, the shade of a smile playing at the corner of his mouth. "And I thought you were just working your way through to Oregon," he said.

"I am." Pike looked over toward Sarah. "But I've got to know that what's past is behind me. We can't make a new life until I do." He got to his feet and looked down at Cassidy. "We've got a big job, boss. Let's hit the hay."

Hopalong Cassidy knew the man, and knew he had as much as he was likely to get. He shrugged, then got to his feet. "All right, but if you know of any good springs back in that nightmare, tell me about them."

"In the morning," he said quietly.

"One thing more. Where's Sipapu?"

Towne hesitated, and for an instant Hopalong did not believe the man would reply, but when he did he spoke quietly. "East of here. It's a ghost town on a trail to nowhere. It's a town that was born quick, lasted only a little while, and then died hard with guns in the streets. It was another place where the vigilante idea didn't work. They hung the crooks, and then each other, and finally died shooting."

His face was twisted with bitterness. "It's a place I've no wish to see, Cameron, nor any man who has ever seen hatred as I saw it in the streets of that town. Hatred and fear."

"You said it was east of here. Just where?"

"You know that trail I mentioned? The one that runs off the Box T road toward the north? That trail used to take you, but it won't anymore because the old canyon bridge is gone. It's just as well. There's no reason for anybody to go, and I don't believe anybody has been there in years."

"Thanks, you've helped me some, Pike. I've got a job here. Pete Melford, the man who owned this land before Tredway showed up, was a friend of mine."

Pike looked at him carefully. "We'll do our best. I've good reason to believe this Colonel Tredway is somethin' different from what he wants everyone to think, and I think he's capable of nearly anything. Of course"—he grinned at Hopalong—"I've reason to think the same way about you." Pike Towne turned and walked to the wagon to join his wife.

Hopalong tossed another stick on the fire and then banked it a little so there would be coals for the morning. Moving back from the flames, he got to his feet and walked to the edge of the woods. The night was very still. The water rustled among the reeds along the banks, the wind stirred, and out in the chaparral there were myriad rustling sounds and stirrings as the creatures of the night came alive for their hunting.

Hopalong Cassidy scowled uncomfortably. He had the feeling of being watched by something he could not see, and he did not like it. He didn't like it at all.

There were things happening about him of which he knew nothing. Pike Towne had been here before, an outlaw, perhaps. Maybe he knew a great deal, and perhaps very little.

He walked on, away from the horses. Behind him the fire dwindled as he moved away until it was scarcely more than another star, glimmering in the night. At last, on a low knoll beside the Picket Fork, he paused. Around him the night was very still. Suddenly a flicker of movement caught his eyes and he looked around. Far away over the top of the chaparral loomed the distant finger of Chimney Butte, pointing at the stars, and then beyond and to the east of it lay Brushy Knoll, a huge, ominous darkness blotting out the distant horizon. Yet he had seen movement there, and now he saw it again, visible at even this distance, the slow movement of lights upon the mountainside!

Cassidy narrowed his eyes, staring into the night. Had there been a trail through the chaparral, he would have saddled up at once, but there was not, so he stood still, watching while the trail of lights mounted higher, and then still higher. At last, after what seemed a very long time, the lights emerged on the very top of the knoll and merged into a group. They flickered there, danced, and held his eyes, and only after a long time did they slowly begin to burn down and vanish. Sobered, he wandered back to the fire. He glanced at his watch and was astonished to see he had been gone for all of two hours!

He crawled into his bed and scarcely felt the ground under him. He sighed, breathed deeply, and was asleep.

Far away, on Brushy Knoll, the lights appeared again, descended in slow, switchback movements until they vanished behind the pear forest. A wind lifted and stirred the leaves, and Topper pricked his ears and stared curiously off into the darkness. At the edge of the dimming firelight, a pack rat crept closer, watched, and sniffed, then moved into camp, curious as always, and alert for something that would interest him enough to steal.

After a long time there was movement in the wagon and then a low question was spoken. The sound, ever so slight, awakened Hopalong. He did not move, but lay very still, listening. At first he could not distinguish the words, and then they began to come through to him.

"No telling what we'll uncover back in there. I'm afraid of it, yet I wouldn't be anywhere else."

Sarah Towne was speaking. "You're not worried, Pike?"

"Of course I'm worried. But what can I do? What else can we do?"

"Suppose he finds out? What will happen?"

There was a long silence, and then Pike's voice, tired now and sounding its worry: "I don't know. Who can know? Kill me, probably, or try it. The trouble is, nobody suspects him. Nobody but me."

"You won't tell them?"

"Tell them? I would tell them nothing! Let them find out!

Of course," he added fatalistically, "he will find out. He's that kind of man."

Nobody spoke for several minutes then, and Hopalong waited, believing they had gone to sleep. Then he began to wonder. Of whom were they talking? Was it Justin Tredway of whom they spoke? What was there he could find out? Why would their presence here be dangerous to Tredway? Or was it he himself of whom they talked?

Pondering this question, Hopalong Cassidy went to sleep.

CHAPTER 4

PAST CRIMES

The big brindle steer backed up and lowered his head as Hopalong turned Topper toward him and shook out a loop. He backed up about three steps and then, as Topper moved in, the steer ducked and bolted for open space. Instantly Hopalong Cassidy dropped his loop. It was a short, easy cast around the horns and the steer jerked to a halt and swung half around. Instantly he charged. Topper swung away, and the jerk of the rope snapped the steer's head around. He stopped, bracing his legs and glaring.

Topper started away from him at once, tugging on the rope. The steer braced himself to resist the unaccustomed tug on his horns and Pike closed in behind on his paint and slapped the steer across the rump with his coiled rope. The steer sprang forward and Topper led off. Pulled from before and struck from behind, the steer went forward reluctantly. He hesitated at the gate of the big corral, but sighting the other cattle inside, he bolted for it. Hopalong brought him up short, then, as the steer turned, Hopalong shook loose his loop and flipped it from the horns.

Freed, the steer raced away toward the others who fed at the far side of the corral. Hopalong mopped the sweat from his face and grinned at Pike. "That's the first one. We've made a start, anyway!"

Pike nodded, rolling a smoke. "Yeah, an' we had a break finding those six head already in the corral. I expect they've been feeding in here ever since it was abandoned."

They turned their horses and started toward the brush. Pike rode without speaking for a short time, and then said unexpectedly, "This Tredway figures to be a sharp dealer. He ain't goin' to like paying us, an' unless our guessin' is wrong, we'll have two thousand dollars comin' before long. We haven't used Shep on this yet, but he'll go back into the deep brush after the worst ones."

"We'll need him there. When they are pushed, these steers will find their way into brush where no man on horseback could go. I don't think Tredway ever figured on a dog."

"If he had"—Pike's voice was thoughtful—"he wouldn't have let us in here. He'd have picked up a dog or two and started in himself."

They rode in silence, then halted at the edge of a new clearing. There were four steers and a cow grazing here. None of them were branded.

Hopalong indicated them with a nod of his head. "Seem funny to you, Pike, that those steers wouldn't be marked? I was thinking that maybe somebody wasn't too sure of himself."

"Looks thataway." Pike drew deep on the stub of his smoke. "You come across by the trail, like we did?"

"Followed your tracks," Hopalong said, waiting to see what Pike Towne had on his mind.

"Country looks mighty dry. Not many cattle back on the reg'lar Box T range. Notice that?"

"I sure did," Hopalong said, "and I'm beginning to wonder a bit. Do you suppose this hombre is as well-off as folks think? That range isn't good. He hasn't made any recent shipments. I've an idea that the Colonel is short of cash. I think he needs these cattle and needs them bad."

"Is that why you don't intend to brand any of them now?"

"Yes, it is," Hopalong said quietly. "Look, Pike. We've been hired for a job. We both have an idea that Tredway may try to run us out of here about the time we get our five hundred head. He won't pay for less, but if he can run us off here before then, he won't have to pay for any.

"All right. We know that. But there's something mighty fishy about all this. I think these cattle weren't branded because, like I said, somebody wasn't too sure of his title to them or if he might not run into a counterclaim. I think he waited to be sure, but now the wait has been long enough, these steers are mostly from four to six years old, the unbranded ones, I mean, and he needs money.

"For all we know, these steers do belong to somebody else. In fact, there's a girl in town now with a cowhand who is trying to locate the old PM brand. It disappeared—the buildings, the cattle, and the owner. So I think we'd better wait and see what happens. We'll put the branded steers in the outer corral where they can be seen, but not many of them."

The work was hot and hard. There was no letup until noon, and by then they had done very little. Their entire morning netted them but six more head, for the cattle had already begun to dodge into the deeper brush.

Taking the afternoon off from the work in the chaparral, Hopalong and Pike went to work to throw up a hurried corral where it could be seen near their camp. They expected no visitors for a few days, and by that time they would drive a few of the tamer, younger cattle or some of the older branded ones to this corral. To aid in the task of driving, they built a chute of poles from the opening in the chaparral to their outer corral. This would prevent any but the wildest steers from breaking away. By the end of the day they had the corral almost completed and part of the line from the chaparral to the corral. They utilized the brush and trees along the way wherever possible. The job was essentially patchwork, but it had no lasting purpose and would serve all immediate needs.

By nightfall, when they gathered up their tools and headed back for the wagon, they were dog-tired. Pike grinned at Hopalong. "Never figured you did this kind of work. I thought you were mainly a rider."

"I have been," Hopalong admitted, "but on the range a man has to turn his hand to a bit of everything."

Sarah's face was flushed from bending over the fire, and she looked up, her eyes lighting with pleasure to see them coming in together. She looked quickly at Pike, and Hopalong caught the expression in her eyes. Sarah Towne might have been worried over her husband returning to his old stomping grounds, but now she was no longer.

"We've had visitors," she said, "and they'll be back. They said they would spend the night with us."

Both men looked up sharply, waiting for her explanation. "It was that pretty girl we saw in Kachina, Pike. Her name is Cindy Blair. She was with a man named Taylor, who works for her."

Hopalong Cassidy relaxed. That was better. He had been afraid it might have been Tredway or Saxx. Either of them would have been suspicious and might have nosed around too much. Hopalong's one hope was to gather most of the cattle back in the brush so they would have well over the required five hundred head before Tredway even dreamed of it. That way they could exact payment from him promptly. Thus far, most of their work had been on corrals and patching up. They had managed to complete more of that than they had expected, but they had done little toward gathering cattle.

They had scarcely begun to eat before they heard the sound of horses and Cindy rode in with Rig. She walked at once to the fire while the cowhand removed the saddles and picketed the horses. She glanced quickly at Hopalong and smiled. "It's good to see you," she said quickly. "If I was short the other night, please forgive me. I was not thinking. My immediate reaction was not to like you because you were working for Tredway."

"Think nothing of it." He made room for her on the log beside him. "What's happening in town?"

"Not much. They are still making inquiries about that old man's death, but they've about given it up as an accident. There's a lot of talk around town, however. Some of it about you."

"Me?" Hopalong looked at her carefully. "What sort of talk?"

"Mostly wondering what was between you two. Several people saw you with him."

"Talking over old times," Hopalong said quietly, and changed the subject. They talked easily after the first few minutes and Hoppy relaxed against the log where he had been sitting and told several stories of the old Texas days while Rig and Cindy listened. She was more than an uncommonly attractive girl, he discovered. She was gifted with a good deal of common sense and more than a little knowledge of the ranching business. After a while, though, he found her looking at him strangely, as if trying to remember something.

"Peavey," he said suddenly, "knew Pete Melford."

"What?" Cindy looked up. "The old man who died."

"I talked to him. I didn't learn much. He knew that Pete was a rancher. What else he knew I have no idea. Tredway came in then and we were interrupted. Old Peavey looked like he saw a ghost, and when I looked up, it was Tredway he was looking at. Tredway called him out with some yarn that somebody wanted to kill Peavey. That was the last time I saw him alive."

"You think Tredway killed him?"

"He may have and may not, but one thing I'll gamble on. He knew him before and liked him none too well."

"Then Tredway saw him talkin' to you?" It was Pike Towne speaking. "I wouldn't call that a favorable sign, my friend."

Hopalong Cassidy shrugged. "No, I wouldn't either. If Tredway had some reason for keeping Melford's past existence a secret, he wouldn't want me around. Nor," he added, more quietly, "my friends here." He nodded to Cindy and Rig.

"You want to remember, Taylor, that hombre I sighted in the brush was shooting at you. He'd waited for a chance, and somebody had told him you were going to be there."

Miles away, in the big ranch house on the Box T, Bill Saxx faced his boss across the table. His eyes were cold and curious. For three years now he had been foreman for Justin Tredway, and before that he had ramrodded a tough bunch of freighters for him, and he had learned more than a little of the man. Tredway possessed a cold, intelligent brain. He was without scruple. He was utterly ruthless when he started after anything or when anything crossed him. He was himself dangerous, Saxx knew. He also knew, or believed, that Tredway would not hesitate to shoot a man in the back if he felt it was the best way. Bill Saxx knew a good deal about Tredway. He never turned his back on him. He told himself now that he never would.

"The boys are kickin', Colonel. They want their money. You owe 'em four months' wages now."

"They'll get it. Tell them not to worry about that!" Tredway's manner was brusque. "Cameron and this man he has helping him are on the job. They'll get those cattle out, or some of them. I've got a market for them right now at twenty dollars a head. That will more than pay them all I owe."

"They don't have much confidence in that," Saxx objected. "You know what happened when we tried gettin' those cows out. We didn't have much luck."

"Cameron's worked in the brush, and I think he's a cow-man. He'll get them out."

Saxx shifted in his chair. "Sure. Maybe they will. The boys sort of had another idea. Not that it would pay their wages, you'd still owe 'em that, but they want money and they want it bad."

"What idea?"

Saxx hesitated, knowing how dangerous it was to suggest anything to this man. Tredway had his own ideas and he was cunning. Usually he was far ahead of you on any idea that was suggested. He seemed to think of everything.

"The payroll for the Taggart Mine," Bill Saxx suggested cautiously.

Tredway stiffened and his face flushed. An angry reply came to his lips, yet even as it formed he stopped it. The Taggart payroll was more than thirty thousand dollars, and he knew as well as anybody did when that payroll was due.

Thirty thousand! Split six ways it was still five thousand apiece, and if he went in as leader, he could demand and get a bigger cut. He sat without replying to Saxx's suggestion, think-ing it over, the possible method, the getaway, the chances of being seen.

"It could be done," he replied cautiously, "but only if it was handled properly."

Bill Saxx relaxed slowly, but within him a suspicion arose, a suspicion that had long lain dormant within him, brought to fresh life by the comparative ease with which Tredway accepted the idea of crime. "Yeah," he said, "the boys figure that payroll must run to twenty thousand dollars."

Tredway hesitated, then realized the first necessity was to impress them with his superior knowledge and planning ability in this field as well as ranching. "Thirty thousand," he said quietly. "I know."

He did not add that old habit had stayed with him and he almost automatically gauged such things, tested and examined them. He did not tell them all he knew, for that could wait. "Unless you planned carefully," he suggested, "you could never swing it. Don't think they haven't considered the possibility of a holdup and what to do in case. They do think of it, and they have plans."

"Such as?" Saxx was watching him alertly. Had the boss been ahead of them on this, too? Had he led them into the suggestion? Or had his thoughts been running with theirs?

"Dead Horse Pass," Tredway replied, smiling a little. "Every time the stage goes through that pass, old Tom Burnside is perched in the rocks up above with a Winchester. Winter or summer, he never fails."

Bill Saxx felt his mouth go dry. That was their plan, to hit that payroll when it came through the pass on the stage. It looked like a sitting duck, whereas had they attempted it, they would themselves be sitting ducks for one of the most deadly old manhunters in the West!

There was only one bit of cover in that pass, and it was no shelter from a rifleman on the cliff above. He could have picked them off one by one, and he could have killed them all! But who would ever have dreamed that Burnside would be up there in the rocks?

"How does that come?" Saxx demanded. "I don't get it."

"Tom Burnside is Patterson's father-in-law," Tredway replied. "When he resigned as deputy down in Cochise County, Patterson invited him to come live with him. Tom wouldn't do it, so Pat offered him this job as a guard on the pass. It was a sort of pension, but he tells me the old man just lives in hopes that some outlaws will try a stickup there so he can justify his job. The old boy has ranged every foot of it, knows just how to hold his sights to kill at any spot, and has tried them all."

Bill Saxx relaxed slowly, worrying. That had been partly his idea. If the boys learned about Burnside, they wouldn't think much of his planning. He looked at Tredway with new respect. "All right," he said, "if not the pass, then where?"

"Just beyond that patch of woods on the Picket Fork. The trail crosses the stream, goes into the woods, then out of them. Just beyond the stream on the right side of the road is part of an old wash, mostly filled with blow sand now, but go back from the trail about sixty yards and there's a deep spot under a bank where a man could conceal his horses. The men could lie in the grass of that filled-in place, all but one."

"What about him?"

"He would come right down the road toward them in plain sight. When he got fairly close, he would hold up a letter to be posted. The stage would pull up to take the letter, and then the boys would close in around it. There wouldn't be a chance in the world of a slipup, and not a shot fired."

Saxx shook his head admiringly. No question about it, the old man was good. The driver might be suspicious going into the pass, and he might be a little suspicious in that patch of woods, but out there on the level? Never! And men were always hailing down the stage to give the driver an order for supplies to be filled by the return stage, or letters to be mailed. It was a cinch.

"Sounds good all right." Saxx leaned over and picked up the can of tobacco and rolled a smoke from it. As he rolled it he turned the whole matter over in his mind. It was quicker money than punching cows, and even if this Cameron did manage to work the cattle out of the pear forest, it would still only be chicken feed. "How about the split?" he asked.

Tredway laid his hands on the table. "Split? One third to me, the rest to the boys."

"One third?" Saxx exclaimed. "That's crazy, boss! An' you do nothin' at all? The boys won't go for it!"

"Then forget it or try it yourself," Tredway replied shortly. "I haven't told you all I know, and by yourselves you'll all wind up dead or in prison. I want one third or no dice."

Bill Saxx leaned back in his chair, scowling. "I'll have to talk it over with 'em. They wanted you in, an' figured you could help. They figured on an even split all around."

"On a basis of twenty thousand dollars? That's unchanged. All I want is ten thousand above the twenty you knew of. If it happens to be less than ten, I'll settle for whatever it is. If it happens to be more, we divide equally."

It was fair enough, Saxx decided reluctantly. Tredway's knowledge had already saved them from being shot down by

Tom Burnside, and there was no telling what else he knew. Tredway had the confidence of all the bigwigs around, and often had dinner with Patterson, who was superintendent at the mine. "I'll put it up to them. I think they'll do it."

At the door he paused. "What about that Cameron, boss? He looks plumb salty. Think he's on the dodge?"

"I wish I knew," Tredway replied honestly. "He has me puzzled."

"What about them out there?"

"Leave them alone for about three or four days. Then take a ride out and see what they've done. They'll be busy for a while, and that's one reason I wanted Cameron out there. I don't want him nosing around town."

"Who do you reckon killed old man Peavey? Think it was Cameron?"

"I doubt it." Tredway looked up from his table. "Where did you get that idea?"

"Folks are talkin' it around. Nobody puts much stock in it, but he was seen with him."

Tredway shrugged. "Not likely, I'd say."

Bill Saxx went out and Colonel Justin Tredway leaned back in his chair. It was the old familiar pattern, but this time it would be different. He would not be riding where the shooting was, he would be sitting back, planning. And he would plan carefully.

He had already made up his mind about what to do to Cameron and the man and wife who helped him. Tredway had seen neither of them, and did not care to. His ideas were clear and sharp. When they had done about all he could get out of them, they would never come out of that brush. It had been a long time since he had been into that chaparral, but he knew a few things about it, a few important things. And there was no better place to dispose of a body . . . who should know that better than he?

During the following days Hopalong and Pike worked hard. It was a grueling, bitter task, and they battled it out through heat, dust, and the stabbing brush. Branches lashed their faces, thorns ripped their shirts, gouged their cheeks. Hopalong rode into town and bought a couple of extra horses, and he broke them to work in the brush. In the outer corral, at the end of the first five days of work, they had thirty head of cattle, all wearing Box T brands, while in the inner corral they had sixty-two head, most of them unbranded. It had been a good beginning, but as the cattle grew wilder it would become increasingly harder to get them out.

Midway of the sixth day they were standing their horses on the edge of one of the small clearings. Only one steer was in sight and he was a rangy black animal that weighed nearly a ton. He was not feeding except for an occasional bit of grass, but he was watching them, his every move showing belligerence. "Huntin' trouble," Pike said, grinning.

In these days of hard work the two men had grown closer together. They understood each other now as only men do who have worked and sweated together and who have learned each to respect the other as a man and a workman.

"What do you think about that place we're using?" Cassidy inquired. "Think it was Ben Hardy's corral?"

Pike shook his head. "No, I don't. He knew of it, I'll bet, because he knew all this country pretty well. The story goes, he knew this brush country better than anybody but one man, one of his own gang."

"Which one was he?"

"Fan Harlan. The name came from his gun fannin', an' he was good at it. Fast as any, an' mighty slick. Last anyone heard of him was when the Hardy gang held up a gold shipment east of Longhorn.

"Hardy was wounded, but he got away. Black John was killed. Nobody ever saw hide nor hair of Harlan, Purdy, or Diego, the other three, again. A lot of folks always figured the posse caught up to 'em, wiped 'em out, an' split the money themselves."

"Much money?"

"Sixty thousand in gold. That's a lot of money, most times."

Pike rolled a cigarette and looked at the black steer with speculative interest. "Lots of rustlers worked this country from time to time. That place, the corral, I mean, it was probably used by rustlers from time to time. But I wouldn't doubt that Harlan knew of it."

Hopalong took his rope from the saddle horn. "You want that one?" He nodded at the black steer. "Or shall I take him?"

Pike Towne grinned. "You take him. I ain't as young as I once was."

Topper moved forward, carrying his head low and looking the belligerent steer right in the eye. The steer didn't like it. He shook his heavy horns and pawed dust with a tentative hoof. He backed up a step, and then, suddenly, he dodged. Instantly Topper was there to meet him, cutting him back toward the open. Then, as the steer wheeled to run, Hopalong's rope shot out like a bullet and whipped around the big horns. The steer hit the end of the rope with a lunge and was jerked from his feet and flopped hard.

He took a minute to get shakily to his feet, but when he got up, the fight was gone out of him. Hopalong turned Topper toward the narrow passage from the clearing, and as the rope tightened, the steer moved forward, hesitantly, wary of the rope.

Halfway down the passage he decided suddenly that he didn't like it. Hopalong, watching over his shoulder, saw the steer gather himself for a sudden charge. There was no chance to maneuver, so he slapped Topper, and the white horse sprang into swift flight with the steer charging after. Topper reached a turn and whipped around it, spinning the steer into the brush. The black steer scrambled to his feet and lunged again, but closing in from behind, Pike nailed him with a second rope and his horse braced himself. The black steer was astonished. Nothing like this had ever happened before, and he found himself pulled from both directions. It took a half hour to get him to the corral, where they turned him loose.

Rig Taylor was loafing at camp when they got there. He looked at Hopalong and grinned. "Can you use another hand?" he asked. "A volunteer? I'd like to see if I've forgotten how to use a rope. Miss Blair has some riding around to do and I think she's getting tired of me."

"We sure could!" Hopalong admitted. "That's tough work. After you catch 'em, they have to be taken through those alleys to the corral. It isn't easy."

"You had a visitor today," Rig commented. "He didn't come down to camp, but he rode along the hillside up there and he looked the place over."

"I was expecting that," Hopalong confessed. He picked up a deep pan and dumped water into it with a gourd dipper and began to splash water on his face and hands. As he washed he considered the unknown watcher. It was probably a hand from the Box T, but it also could have been the man who first shot at Rig.

Leaving Rig Taylor to work at the wide northern part of the chaparral, Hopalong took a winding opening in the brush that led to the east. Pike and Rig could work together, and he would move out by himself. He was well started before he sighted Shep. The dog loped up to him, grinning happily and wagging his tail, fairly begging not to be sent back.

"All right, Shep, we'll work together. First we'll get an idea where this goes. That will be something to know. Plenty of cow tracks, anyway."

The tangle grew fiercer, and several times Shep yipped when stabbed by thorns he inadvertently brushed against. At points the wall of the pear forest closed in so tightly that the ugly spines thrust out with barely space enough to work a way through.

Rounding a tight corner in the alley between the prickly pear, a big, mouse-colored steer suddenly loomed not a dozen yards ahead of them. Had their appearance been a moment less instantaneous than it was, it might have been dangerous. As it happened, their sudden appearance so startled the animal that he threw up his head and, rearing, turned almost completely around on his hind feet, and led off in a lunging run.

Aware that he might stop at any moment and decide to fight, Hopalong took a chance. If he could keep the steer running! Topper saw only a running steer and it was his job to chase and round them up, and he knew his job. Springing from a standing start, Topper darted after the steer. A branch—luckily it was only mesquite—slapped Cassidy across the face, and then they rounded a bend and the steer wheeled off the narrowing track and hurled himself squarely at the wall of brush!

Surprisingly, it gave with his weight and he plunged through. Topper waited for no orders. Turning so sharply that Hopalong might have touched the ground with his foot, he dashed after the steer. The lunge carried them through whipping branches, and something slashed Hopalong along the arm, and then they were through and into what a few years before must have been a clearing but was now covered by a beginning growth of chaparral.

The mouse-colored steer was heading across it, tail up and running. Hopalong swung Topper to avoid a bristling barrel cactus and then the steer was running full tilt at the wall of brush. Yet here, too, he must have known where he was going, for he plunged through into a still-larger clearing. Shep dashed on ahead, circling to get ahead of the steer, and then, past the head of the horse, beyond the running steer, Hopalong saw something else. It was a low cabin or shelter!

Reining in the eager horse, he stood in his stirrups and looked over the tops of the young brush. Here where he now was there had not long ago been a large clearing, but already the chaparral was claiming it. Yet the cabin, old as it was, still stood.

The steer ran on and away, but Hopalong called back the dog and then moved cautiously forward. His hand went back to his pistol and slid off the leather thong that bound it in place while brush-riding.

Several times he drew to a halt, listening. There was no sound but the low wind, scarcely discernible in the thick brush. On the edges of the clearing, giant pear stood up eight or nine feet, a fierce entanglement denying all entry or exit to the clearing for most of its circumference. There was no path, no trail.

The shelter itself was built of logs and had a pole roof, heavily thatched. The lower walls, however, had been piled high with rock, obviously for defense. Somewhere Hopalong Cassidy heard water running.

Suddenly he stopped dead still.

An old corral had fallen away, only the posts and a few rotting poles left, but on the ground where the gate must have been was a whitening skull!

Hopalong moved nearer and saw the skull was only a few feet from the scattered remains of a skeleton. The leather gun belt was stiff as iron, the heavy guns rusted. One bony hand was still clasped to a gun that had never been drawn. The hole through the skull was adequate explanation.

Hopalong swung down and bent over the body. A leather scabbard, dried and stiff with age, was affixed to the belt. There was no knife in the scabbard. This man had been shot from behind, the small hole in the back of the head and the smashed frontal bone of the head proved that. The walnut butt plates on the six-shooters were carved with a large letter *D*.

Turning away from the skeleton, Hopalong moved toward the dark opening of the cabin. The door had long since fallen from its crude leather hinges and it lay flat upon the ground. Evidently it had been left ajar.

Stepping to the door, Hopalong peered in, then froze, startled at what he saw. Another skeleton lay collapsed against the far wall!

His face pale, Hopalong struck a match. Within was a table with a candle stuck in the neck of a bottle. Its sides were covered with tallow from the candle drippings, and obviously it had seen much use. Hopalong touched his match to the wick and as the flame sprang up, lighting again after so long a time, he looked around.

There was a heavy stone fireplace, a table, two crude benches, hastily and awkwardly made, and two tiers of bunks, enough for four men at least. Then he turned his eyes to the skeleton.

It lay with its back to the door, one bony hand clutching a rusty rifle. Moving closer, Hopalong saw a long-bladed knife had gone in through its left side right below the fifth rib and slanting slightly upward. Examining the log wall, he could see where the point of the knife had sunk in at least two inches before the weight of the corpse had pulled it free!

For an hour Hopalong wandered about, studying the room, examining everything in it. Some ancient burlap in a corner, stiff now, but still holding its former shape, completed the picture. Unless all his conclusions were wrong, Hopalong Cassidy knew that this was the final scene in the long-ago robbery of a shipment from the mines. The gold bars had been wrapped in that burlap, and three men had come here, to this place, before their greed had played its final hand.

No doubt each of these men was thirsting for possession of all the gold. Black John lay dead back at the scene of the robbery. Probably they thought Ben Hardy was also, for the story was that he had been badly wounded and they had probably seen him shot. That meant sixty thousand to split three ways, but without doubt each was thinking—why not only one way?

Possibly this conclusion maligned the man whose skeleton lay there against the wall. Maybe he had wanted to await the possible return of Ben Hardy. Maybe he had merely been the unfortunate one to die. The knife was carved with the name Diego, and it was the knife from the scabbard of the skeleton outside.

The three had come here, and Diego had awaited his chance. A hard-thrown knife had done the work as soon as the man turned his back. Perhaps he was placing his rifle on those nails, perhaps he was taking it down. In any event, the knife had settled that. And then Diego had gone to the corral after horses, and he, in turn, had been shot. The survivor had ridden away with sixty thousand dollars in gold!

A stiff leather wallet, fallen from rat-gnawed clothing, identified the second man. The first part of the name was obliterated, but the last name was Purdy.

Then the missing man with the sixty thousand dollars and the murder of his friends on his soul was Fan Harlan!

Hopalong Cassidy walked outside. A faint breeze somehow found the clearing and dried the sweat on his face. He looked around, and Topper nickered. The white horse was standing over a pool of water and Shep was panting contentedly beside him, lying on the hard-packed earth.

Crossing to them, he found a pool all of twenty feet across, the water flowing from a crack in the rocks of an ancient outcropping, evidently part of the same ledge by which Hopalong had originally found entrance to the chaparral. There was plenty of water for cattle, and their tracks proved that they came here often. There were deer tracks, too, and one track that might have been a mountain lion. This was somewhat smudged, however.

Measuring with a stick, Hopalong found the pool to be all of five feet deep and the water quite clear. This, then, was an all-year water hole, but was patronized by only a small portion of the wild cattle. That indicated there was water elsewhere, either easier of access or greater in extent.

No sound came to him but the slight trickling of water and the panting of the dog. Hopalong Cassidy walked back to the house and looked around. Without doubt the killer had never returned to this spot; if so, he had touched nothing. No doubt he was long gone from the country with his ill-gotten gains. But was he? Was he still around or had he just returned?

Suddenly he heard a voice!

Stepping back into the deep shadow under a gnarled old pin oak, he stared toward the opening in the brush through which he had come. Waiting, he touched his tongue to his lips. Shep was on his feet and then, wagging his tail, dashed into the brush.

He heard the voice again, then a reply, and over the tops of the pear and chaparral he saw two riders.

Rig Taylor and Pike Towne. He heard Towne greet the dog and then the two men pushed through the brush into the clearing. As Hopalong Cassidy stepped out to meet them he suddenly realized that he very much wanted to watch Pike's face when he looked around.

The two men rode forward. Suddenly Rig Taylor pointed. "Blazes, man! Look at that!" He was pointing toward the skeleton of Diego.

Pike slid from the saddle no more than sixty feet from Hopalong and stood staring down at the remains. When he looked up, he started at once for the cabin. His face was cold and ugly.

"No need to look, Pike. I can tell you. The one who came out alive was Fan Harlan."

Shocked, he stared at Cassidy, his face drawn. "How . . . ? How do you know that?"

"Figured it out. They came here after that holdup. Had some kind of a mix-up. Diego threw a knife into Purdy and nailed him to the wall inside. He's still there. When he came outside a third man it seems would've had to have been Fan Harlan shot him in the back of the head. You saw the skull."

"Yeah." Pike Towne's face was cold and hard. "Guess you got it figured. I—I all us had an idea the three were wiped out by the law, or maybe they took out all together."

Rig Taylor stared from one to the other, puzzled and curious. "I don't get this," he said. "Who were these guys?"

Hopalong Cassidy replied. "Outlaws. Pike and I were talking about it earlier. The Ben Hardy gang; they robbed a gold shipment from a mine. They got shot up, but three of them disappeared. Now we know they were killed . . . or two of them were."

Taylor relaxed slowly, his searching eyes on Hopalong's face. "So this Fan Harlan is the only one who survived?"

"No, Ben Hardy was wounded and sent to prison," Hopalong said casually. "No one knows where he is now."

CHAPTER 5

GHOST TOWN TRAIL

There was little talk during the ride back as each of the three was occupied with his own thoughts. What they were thinking Hopalong had no idea, nor was he wondering. He was busy with the problem of the two living outlaws. One of them had gotten away with sixty thousand dollars, the other was alive somewhere and by now might know exactly what had happened. All of which did not spell happiness for Fan Harlan or his sixty thousand, if he still had it.

Riding out of the chaparral, the first thing Hopalong saw was Bill Saxx. The big foreman wore a dark blue shirt and black jeans. His hat was off, and his heavy shock of blond hair identified him at first glance. He was standing across the fire from Cindy Blair.

"No," he was saying, "you're on the wrong track. There was never any Pete Melford in this country. The old man must have been yarnin' or else you got your directions wrong."

"We've got visitors," Hopalong whispered, just loud enough for the others to hear.

"How can you be so sure?" Cindy's voice sounded irritated. "You didn't come into this country until shortly after my uncle was killed—or I don't believe you did."

"What do you mean by that?" Saxx demanded sharply.

"As a matter of fact," Hopalong said loudly as he rode up, "Saxx was here when Melford was killed."

Saxx turned sharply, staring at Hopalong, then from him to the others. It was obvious that he liked none of this. He had not expected to find them in, and if so, not more than two men.

"Saxx wasn't foreman of the Box T, though," Hopalong continued easily. "He was ramrodding Tredway's freight outfit for him. When the Colonel went to ranching, he took Saxx with him."

"You seem to know a lot!" Saxx sneered.

"I just keep my ears open." Hopalong smiled reassuringly at Sarah Towne, who stood wide-eyed and fearful beyond the fire.

Bill Saxx was watching Hopalong, making no effort to conceal the dislike in his eyes. "What business is all this to you?" he said sharply. "What you stickin' your nose in for?"

Hopalong Cassidy looked around at him. "Aside from the fact that I want to help Miss Blair, it so happens that Pete Melford was a friend of mine."

Cindy stared at Hopalong, frowning a little. Rig was suddenly alert, and Pike Towne was smiling mysteriously. Saxx was astonished, and then his face seemed to go still and tight. His mind was moving swiftly. Tredway should know this. He had not suspected—or had he? There was no telling about the Colonel.

"I didn't know you'd been in this country before."

"I never was," Cassidy admitted, accepting the cup Sarah offered him. "I knew Pete in Texas. He wrote a letter to me, asking me to come by, but that letter was years late being delivered. It begins to look like I was quite a bit too late to help him. But I'm not too late to help Cindy Blair."

"Why didn't you say so?" Rig demanded irritably.

"No need to," Hopalong said. "I figured it might be a good thing just to be around and be busy. There would be plenty of time later."

"Well," Bill Saxx snapped, "it's time wasted! There never was any Pete Melford in this country! If anybody would know, I would."

Hopalong smiled, and the smile infuriated Saxx. His eyes narrowed and he glared at Cassidy. "You huntin' trouble?" he demanded harshly.

"Me?" Hopalong's eyebrows lifted in surprise. "I should say not! I'm just a quiet hombre myself. But"—he tried the coffee and found it too hot—"I am going to locate Miss Blair's ranch, and it will be in her hands when I leave.

"No trail," he added, "is so well covered that it cannot be uncovered."

Pike Towne had walked away to the wagon, but now he was back. He was wearing two guns, tied down, and it was the first time Hopalong had seen him wear a pistol. Suddenly Hoppy's eyes sparked. Pike Towne was ready to stand his ground, that was obvious.

That the Box T hands saw the guns and recognized what they meant was also obvious. None of the other hands had spoken, although Carter had been staring with hatred in his eyes, mostly at Hopalong.

Bill Saxx looked the situation over and decided it was time to pull out. He knew he must contact Tredway at once with this latest information, but before he did that Saxx wanted to do some thinking on his own. Just where this left him was important to know; for the first time he was becoming wary of Tredway's plans.

Right now any move might be disastrous to their plans for the holdup of the Taggart payroll only three days away. Saxx motioned to the other hands to come along and turned away. "Well"—he forced himself to smile—"regardless of trails, lots of luck with the cattle. You've got a tough job!"

"Oh, I was never so glad to see anybody in my life!" Cindy exclaimed as Saxx and his men disappeared into the distance. "They acted so strange! That man called Carter. He was asking all sorts of questions and looking around, and all the time Bill Saxx talked to us, the others were out at the corral looking at the cattle, reading their brands."

"Saxx seemed to think you should have more done," Sarah said. "He should try it himself!"

Pike grinned slyly at Hopalong. "Or have a look back in the brush."

"I didn't know you were a friend of Pete Melford's," Rig protested. "I had no idea you knew him."

Pike leaned against the rock and speared a chunk of beef from the pot and listened carefully.

"Well, he had to be careful, Rig," Cindy said. "Too much talk might have given him away."

"Given what away? What do you mean?"

"Uncle Pete always used to tell us stories about his neighbors in Texas." She was smiling at Hopalong. "Anybody who heard them would know who Mr. Cameron was." She looked to Rig, waiting for him to understand. "Most of those stories were about one ranch, the Bar-20."

"The Bar-20?" Rig Taylor stared at Hopalong. "Then—then you're Hopalong Cassidy!"

Pike chuckled. "Sure he is! I guessed it right off!"

A dark figure rose suddenly from the tall grass under the poplars and glided swiftly back into even deeper shadows. Tote Brown had been planning for a shot at Rig Taylor, but now he knew that he had something infinitely more important for the man who hired him. He was not sure how soon the news would get to him, but he wanted it to be soon.

As he rode, his mind worked swiftly. Suppose his deductions were correct and the mysterious messages came from Tredway? And who else stood to gain by the death of Taylor? Or of any of them, for that matter?

He would take a chance. He would take a big chance. He would see that Tredway got the news of Cassidy's presence at once. If Tredway was his man, then all would be well. If not, what harm could it possibly do? And it might earn him a fat bonus.

*   *   *

Justin Tredway sat at his desk in the huge ranch house studying a carefully drawn map. Had Bill Saxx seen that map, he would have been amazed, for it was a map, drawn in meticulous detail, of the area from Dead Horse Pass to the wash east of the stage route. On the map was marked every depression, every boulder and tree in the area, and Tredway was studying it and thinking.

Once the pattern of a man's life is established, it is rarely, if ever, changed. The character of a man is not a variable thing, but it follows in certain grooves cut long ago in youth. So it was with the man known as Tredway. He had begun by living ruthlessly, caring for none but himself, without loyalty, without honor, and with only a fierce pride in his own skill, intelligence, and personality.

Just as he had left behind him all sympathy for anyone or anything, so he had left behind him all respect for courage. The idea did not interest him, for so many brave men so easily become dead men. He prided himself on his efficiency. That there were blind spots in himself he did not see. Like most men of criminal tendency, he saw only his own viewpoint and had nothing but contempt for the minds of others. He could play any role; in fact, taking on false lives and personalities appealed to him in such a way that he sometimes forgot who he had been for days or even weeks at a time.

It had been a long time since he had come down that trail from Chimney Butte, a long time since things happened there.

That he was here at all was, he understood himself well enough, an act involved to show his contempt.

That trail from Chimney Butte had carried him a long way, but he had come back, and he had found the old buildings at the settler's stopover deserted as he had known he would. The new mines opened were crying for freight, and he gave it to them, and more. He built a freight and stage station and called it Kachina; the town started from that beginning. He had opened a general store and made Kachina the supply point for the mines and ranches. His teams fed on hay from his own ranches, and quiet and safe years had passed.

But lately there had been trouble. A heavily loaded freight wagon had gone off a cliff, killing the team and the driver. The load had been dumped into the creek and he had been liable for it. A hard winter caught most of the cattle in high country, and an unexpected snowstorm prevented their removal. Many of them failed to survive the bitter season that followed, and it was a winter Tredway had spent in El Paso and San Antonio. He returned to find himself nearly broke. A fiercely hot and very dry summer followed and more cattle died and feed ran short.

His bank accounts depleted, bills for feed, three new teams, and wagons coming due as well as various other bills, Tredway turned first to the idea of getting the cattle out of the chaparral. Saxx's suggestion as to grabbing the Taggart payroll had come at just the right time for him. Actually, he had known about the payroll long before Saxx approached him, and at the time he had been wondering how to suggest it to him.

He had no money with which to pay Cameron for the cattle, but neither had he any intention of paying it. Cameron was a stranger, and he was not going to win any friends around this town while he was getting cattle out of the brush. Moreover, the vague suspicion that he might have had something to do with the death of old Peavey might be worked into something, if necessary.

Cindy Blair was more of a problem. Western men were notoriously particular about how a woman was treated, and Cindy, slim, erect, and attractive, had made more than a few friends around—friends she did not even know about herself. Her frank friendliness, good cheer, and willingness to ride at all hours and over all kinds of country appealed to these men. Even Bill Saxx had said something about her being pretty.

From what he had been told, both she and Rig Taylor were now at the cattle-hunting camp on the Picket Fork. He scowled and went back to his work. Maybe he had been a fool ever to suggest getting those cattle out.

With the map before him, he was studying the layout of the holdup situation. Bill Saxx was to flee northeast, then circle, passing near Babylon Mesa and meeting him at Sipapu. If all was well, they could then return to the ranch. It was at that point that Justin Tredway thought of an alternative. His eyes narrowed with thought, he leaned back in his chair, considering every possibility. Yes, he decided, it might be done. With planning, it could be done.

At just that instant a rock sailed through the open window, struck his desk, skidded along it, and fell into his lap.

Springing to his feet, he whipped out his gun and stepped away from the light, staring out of the open window from a position well back inside the room.

There was no sound, and he waited a long minute, then another. To his ears came faintly, the distant beating of a horse's hooves, then silence. Curious, he walked back to his desk and picked up the rock.

It was flat and quite heavy, and it had been tossed rather than thrown into the room. Tied to it was a piece of brown wrapping paper such as was used at the general store in Kachina. Untying it, he unfolded the paper. The message was crudely printed but explicit enough.

CAMERON IS HOPALONG CASSIDY, FRIEND OF PM

For several long minutes Justin Tredway did not move, and when finally he became aware of his surroundings, the first thing he noticed was the ticking of the clock. In the empty room the sound was loud and clear. He shook himself and stared again at the brown paper.

Hopalong Cassidy.

Hopalong Cassidy was here, he had been in Kachina. He was even now hunting cattle for the Box T. It seemed incredible, impossible, but there it was. It was not in Tredway to doubt, for once the name was mentioned, he realized how obvious it had been. Melford was from Texas and had a long association with the Bar-20 Ranch, an operation where, for many years, Bill "Hopalong" Cassidy had been foreman.

How had he come here? Why had he come here? What was happening that he, Tredway, did not know?

In the light of this information, all plans would have to be reconsidered, for Cassidy had always been on the side of the law, and the man was no fool. He had proved before this that he was uncommonly shrewd, that he read sign well, and certainly that he could handle a gun.

Suddenly a chill went over Tredway. Suppose—suppose Cassidy found what had stayed hidden for so many years back there in the chaparral? Tredway forced himself to sit down and think coolly. Suppose he did? Nobody in town knew anything. Cassidy had talked to Peavey, but Peavey was dead and buried now, and he had known little, in any event. Would Cassidy wait for evidence? Tredway did not know.

But suppose—suppose the fleeing bandits happened to run into Hopalong?

Suppose Bill Saxx, Vin Carter, and the others encountered Hopalong as they fled the holdup scene? Carter would not hesitate to kill, and for that matter, neither would the others. Five men against Cassidy, especially when one of them was Bill Saxx? Tredway smiled.

It could be arranged, of course, but that meant that he, Tredway, must get his hands on the money first or it would be of no use. If the loot was still in the hands of the outlaws and anything went wrong, it might be lost to him, for they might leave the country with his share, or someone might hear the shots and get to the scene before he could.

Of course, he reflected, if it did come to shooting, it was possible that all might be wiped out, all or most of them. And it could be arranged that none survived. The more he considered that possibility, the better it seemed. Thirty thousand was much better than ten, and suppose when the shooting started, he himself were bedded down nearby with a rifle?

The rifle had always been a favorite weapon with him, and he had been a dead shot since boyhood. During a fight nobody would know where the bullets all came from, and if there were any survivors . . . Well, there would be no survivors.

Drawing the light nearer, he carefully burned the note and then began to study the map. He had been working over it for twenty minutes before he received his next jolt, and he was shocked that he had not thought of it before.

Who had thrown the note through the window? Who knew that he would want to know that Cameron was Cassidy?

Suppose it was Cassidy himself? He considered that, then dismissed the idea. Hopalong Cassidy would have nothing to gain by such an action. Who else, then?

Definitely worried, he got up and began to pace the floor. His own men would have come to him at once. The man who worked with Cassidy? He had never seen the man—a married man with a wagon, they said, a passing stranger.

Cindy Blair? It was an outside chance. The girl was clever, she had shown that by her businesslike attitude. She was dangerous, too, because she made friends.

Tote Brown? He puzzled over that possibility, then dismissed it. Regardless of who had supplied the information, he had to come up with a plan and he had to pull it off in a place where he would be free of interference.

Sipapu. The ghost town occurred to him at once. That was the logical place. All thought of the unknown messenger dismissed from his mind, he began at once to study the methods he might use if Sipapu was to be the scene of a fight between Cassidy and Saxx.

It was logical enough, for Saxx would be taking his men that way on the day of the holdup. An anonymous note could get Cassidy and his friends there also, and with no love lost between them, Saxx would be sure to believe they had been discovered. Vin Carter hated Cassidy and had a hair-trigger temper. Shooting was inevitable, and he knew just the place he could hole up to handle the survivors.

The following day Cindy Blair mounted her horse, determined to do some looking for the site of the PM without interference. Hopalong would be working in the brush with Rig and Pike and they would be safely out of the way, giving her a chance to have a look for the site of the ranch.

Rig had given her a complete account of his experiences when he had first encountered Hopalong Cassidy on what he had believed was the site of the PM Ranch, so now Cindy turned her mare in that direction and in a short time was riding down the slope along which Hopalong had ridden after taking his shot at Tote Brown.

The valley was green and lovely, for despite the dryness of the year, the waters of the Picket Fork all drained into this area, and there were several small brooks that started from springs back in the trees and rocks. With Pete Melford's letter in her hand, she drew up and looked about. On the letter was a crude sketch, and turning her horse, she turned the sketch until it was oriented with the landmarks on the ground. Brushy Knoll and

Chimney Butte were exactly as he had said, and the Picket Fork cut across the range just as on the map. Right now she should be sitting her horse not more than two hundred yards from the ranch house.

Turning her mare again, she studied the terrain where the ranch was supposed to be if her sketch was correct. To her left was a lightning-blasted stump, and that, too, was on her sketch, but nothing else was the same. Where the ranch house should have been was a tall cottonwood, and where the barns should be there was a small grove of pines.

The pines were young, but they were not that young. They could be no less than eight or nine years old. Puzzled, she rode forward and swung down from her horse. Standing under the spreading limbs of the cottonwood, she looked back where the corrals should have been, then paced off the distance.

With a long branch she found lying nearby, Cindy began to probe the ground. If there had been a corral, there had been postholes, and when filled, these are rarely packed down. She worked steadily but without success. Grass had grown over everything, and the trees . . . Suddenly her stick sank through soft earth, and with a little cry Cindy dropped to her knees. In an instant she was digging earth from a round hole, its edges firm and hard with ancient sod. She had found a posthole! It was the first definite clue.

*   *   *

To work brush a man not only had to be an excellent rider but a superb hand with a rope. There was no chance to build a loop. Often all a man saw was a fleeting glimpse of a hoof, and it was a short rope, a quick throw, or nothing.

Leather tapaderas housing the stirrup were an essential. A stiff branch might run through an open stirrup, leaving the cowhand with a torn or broken leg, a lost stirrup, or a badly gouged horse. At the very least he could have his saddle torn from under him in full flight. Brush cattle were usually larger than on open range, for they might go years and never see a cowhand, and usually they knew places where water and grass were plentiful.

More often than not, there were no holes in the brush and a cowhand hit it flat and hard, tearing an opening by sheer drive. He went through with thorns ripping his clothes, branches slapping or stabbing at him, and literally forced a way through. Brutally hard work, it required a brand of riding and toughness demanded by no other craft.

"Let's get Shep busy," Hopalong suggested. "We can work him every day from now on. We want to finish this job fast, and remember, what I want most is a PM brand."

He had seen Cindy leaving camp and was worried. Yet he knew she was a cow-country girl and had unusually good judgment. However, no amount of judgment will stop a bullet, and he had a better than fair idea of what they were coping with. Hopalong was sure that both Saxx and Tredway knew more about Pete Melford than they would admit, and he was sure now that the attempt to kill Rig had come because his refusal to leave was worrying whoever it was who did know the facts.

Hopalong pushed into the thickest brush, turning steers

toward the clearings to be roped. Many would not be led or driven and consequently had to be tied tightly abreast of one of Pike's oxen. Calm, wise, and powerful, the oxen knew exactly what to do. As Pike Towne had driven six oxen into the country, they used them all, three each day on alternate days. All of them had done this sort of work in Texas and knew well what was expected of them. Invariably they started at once for the home corral when tied to a wild steer, and fight as the wild one might, he was taken along. Such steers have been known to fight to the death, but the ox is usually the heavier, the more stubborn, and he knows what he is doing. As a result he wins most often.

Rig Taylor was a top hand. He had done little brush work before, but enough to get the feel of it, and he threw himself into it with everything he had. Cindy Blair had forgotten she was owner of a ranch and had fallen in beside Sarah Towne and was helping the older woman prepare their meals.

The use of the dog and the three oxen made the work much easier, and some of the younger stuff could actually be herded out. By nightfall more than sixty head had been brought in, the branded stock being thrown into the outer corral, the unbranded held in the hidden corral back in the brush.

The following day they started again, and worked so far toward the north that on several occasions Hopalong found himself almost on the edge of Chimney Creek Canyon, with the towering six-hundred-foot rim of Babylon Mesa facing him about two miles beyond.

Chimney Creek Canyon was unbelievably wild and desolate. The brush gave way to lower-growing varieties strongly mingled with sage, and then to a few cedar and piñon along the rim. The canyon was deep, seemingly offering no possible route to the bottom, and an impassable barrier to further movement to the north. Seized by a sudden urge for exploration, Hopalong pushed free of the brush and began working his way along the rim toward the east.

He had ridden for several miles when he drew up to let Topper catch his breath and, turning in his saddle, looked back. He was just in time to catch the blinking of a mirror from the higher slopes of Brushy Knoll!

Somebody was signaling, and to someone who must be ahead of Hopalong.

When Hopalong moved on, it was not to return to camp. Instead, he rode rapidly along the canyon rim toward the site of the bridge. When he arrived, it was late afternoon and the sun was making its way down, toward the rim of the mountains. He sat under cover of the trees looking across the narrow canyon, studying the ruins of Sipapu.

Only five buildings remained intact. All were obviously store buildings of one kind or another, but one might have been a hotel or rooming house. There were the ruins of a dozen other buildings within sight, but no sign of life in the town. He watched it for a time, and when he was positive there was nobody within the town, he dismounted and picketed Topper on the rich grass in a small glade within the forest.

Habitually he carried a long, California-style reata. During the brush work he had been using a thirty-five-foot rope, but the reata, such as the old vaqueros had used, was all of seventy-five feet long. Now he took it down from the saddle and walked to the rim of the canyon. He wanted a look at the town and had no idea of riding clear around to the bridge, which would take him at least a day, owing to the rugged terrain and thick chaparral.

Opposite him was a bridge post that looked as sturdy as the day it was put in. He took care to examine it with his glasses before making his attempt.

The canyon at this point narrowed to no more than fifty feet wide, and the cast, while not easy, was to a large, stationary target. Pulling the noose tight, he made his own end fast to a tree, and then slipping the thongs over his guns so they would not fall out, he lay down on top of the rope. One leg he kept outstretched along the rope, the rope running inside the knee and outside the foot. His left leg hung straight down as a balance. Then he pulled himself, hand over hand, across the canyon. It was much the simplest way of crossing anywhere or anything on a rope, and it was a method he had used before on more than one occasion.

Getting to his feet on the opposite side of the canyon, Hopalong made his way slowly back to the trail that ran off the fallen-in bridge.

A movement caught his eye, and he looked up to see a man step soundlessly from the trees along the path. Bearded, the man wore his hair long and was dressed in a homespun garment of brown that fell around him like a mantle with long sleeves. It was gathered at the waist with a rawhide belt, woven of many strands.

The man eyed him without speaking, and seemed unarmed but for the staff he carried and a knife at his belt.

"You are a stranger here?" The bearded man spoke with a soft yet clear voice.

"Yes," Hopalong replied. His curiosity was aroused, but he knew this must be one of the strange sect who lived atop Babylon Mesa. "You are from Babylon Pastures?"

"Yes. And you are working cattle in the brush? For whom do you work?"

Hopalong watched him closely. "Contracting," he said, "but the cattle are Colonel Tredway's."

"Do you plan to work north of the canyon?"

"Hadn't figured on it," Hopalong admitted. "I'm just having a look around."

"I wondered. We have seen a man looking around at Sipapu. We thought it might be one of you. We do not," he continued, "look with pleasure on people coming north of the canyon. For a number of years now we have lived in almost complete isolation, and that is the way we like it. Our beliefs are not the beliefs of others, and it is better if we are left alone."

Hopalong nodded. "Your beliefs are none of my business, that's the way I see it. A man is free to do what he wants to do as long as he doesn't interfere with another man's freedom or way of doing things."

"We have been curious," the man said. "There has been much strange riding in the past few days. We keep," he added, "a careful lookout. There has been a good deal of activity along the stage road. Two men have ridden from it out toward Sipapu. One of them ran his horse as if pursued from the stage road toward Sipapu. It was very peculiar, for no one was behind him."

His eyes suddenly alert, Hopalong Cassidy considered this.

A man prowling around Sipapu, others along the old stage road, and one of them running his horse? That sounded like someone planning a holdup.

The idea seemed farfetched, yet when all was considered, why else would a man be running a horse from the stage route into a wild and remote section of the country? Perhaps he was timing the trip to see how long it would take and the best route.

The bearded man nodded. "The rider crossed the Picket Fork on the main-trail bridge, went on up the road toward an old wash, and then from near there raced to Sipapu."

"If you don't mind," Hopalong said, "I'll have a look around Sipapu." He turned to the bearded man. "What do you call your outfit?"

"We have no name," the bearded man said, "except that we refer to ourselves as the Brothers. In origin we were once allied to the Franciscan order, but we disagreed and under our prophet, Logan, we left and set up our own colony." He hesitated, then looked gravely at Hopalong. "You have heard of the Penitentes? We are an offshoot of theirs."

He smiled slightly. "The Brothers would not like me to phrase it that way, but such is the case. Our belief is simple, and we keep to ourselves, till our fields, raise a few goats; we live simply but well."

"And have a good signal system," Hopalong said, chuckling.

The bearded man laughed. "You are observant. Yes, we have had to have. At first there was some Indian trouble, then outlaws, and now we wish to avoid outside contacts, and consequently we keep careful watch on all movements around us.

As a result we have become very skilled in understanding the movements of men who are on business of their own. When we see something like today, we are naturally puzzled."

For more than an hour they talked. Hopalong had learned that long ago the sect had been more open in their contact with outsiders. But following the chaos that had caused Sipapu to be abandoned, they had discovered that people in the area, especially those devout in other faiths, felt that they were somehow evil and therefore responsible for the curse that had fallen over the small community. The Brothers then retreated to their mesa and severed most of their contacts with the outside world. They had known Pete Melford, however. In fact, the old Texan had been quite friendly with them and had been one of the few to visit them up on the mesa.

Finally the Brother announced that he had to be going. "It is good," he told Hopalong, "to talk to an outsider who does not fear or shun us. It does not happen often." He moved off into the brush near the base of the slope, a mysterious, but somehow lonely figure.

Hoppy walked toward the ruins of Sipapu. Two of the buildings before him were of stone, one of adobe, the others of crude lumber. This lumber had now aged silver brown, and the shutters on the windows hung on ancient hinges. Pete Melford had mailed his letter from here over three years ago. Given the condition of the place, it hardly seemed possible that it was even that recently, although Hopalong had gathered that it had been practically deserted even then.

The shadows were black under the rim of Babylon Mesa, and he walked slowly, studying the town as he approached. The first building was a frame structure and he stepped to the door and peered in. The floor was a litter of ancient papers, broken glass, and a few scattered bottles. The ceiling had partly fallen in and there was a broken chair.

Withdrawing, he walked on to the second of the buildings. It had been a saloon, and the mirror in the bar back was still intact. There were many empty bottles here, a long bar in good shape, and some scattered and ancient playing cards. There were tables and a few chairs, a stove that was still good, and even a pile of wood for burning.

His footsteps sounded hollowly on the hard floor. He found himself pausing to listen intently as one so often does in an empty building. A glass still stood on the bar, and Hopalong had started past it when he jerked to a halt.

That glass had been used!

Not only had it been used, but within a matter of an hour or so! Far from having dust on it, there was even a drop of moisture in the bottom!

An eerie feeling crept over Hopalong and he stared around uncomfortably, watching on all sides. No sound. Cobwebs trailed across the windows and over a doorway to an upper story. Broken glass on the floor, and dust. A boot print in the dust—his own? No sound. The old building creaked. A hot gust of wind blew down the empty street, a ghost wind stirring the tall grass and ruffling leaves.

The room grew dark. He walked to the door and stared out into the silence. As the sun set, the shadow of the mesa had moved across the street to cover all but the tops of the buildings. From somewhere voices were heard, singing—voices from high up on the rim. A rat scurried across the street. A rabbit hopped near the fallen poles of the old corral. Ghosts moved and communed in Sipapu—the ghosts of men who had walked, belted and booted, down this narrow street, who swaggered into these saloons, drinking at these bars. But who had emptied the glass that now stood on the bar? Where had he come from?

Dusk obscured the room, but from somewhere a vagrant light came and caught the glass and held it, shining slightly, a little apart from everything on the bar. Hopalong's flesh crawled and involuntarily his hand dropped to his gun. He stepped out on the empty street and felt eyes watching him. Or was he dreaming it?

He walked slowly toward the next building and entered it. Again there was nothing, but still he felt the watching eyes. Could it be the Brother from Babylon Pastures? Or was it the mysterious rider who had come dashing out of the broken country to the dead town?

He stepped out the door, and then something slapped the doorjamb beside him and a gun roared in the stillness of the approaching night. Jerking back, he drew in one fast flowing motion and stood waiting for the next move, his heart pounding. Nothing more happened, and he moved. Instantly the next shot came, and then with slow and methodical effort the unknown marksman began to shoot the building full of holes.

First he smashed at the top of Hopalong's head, but Cassidy dropped to his face on the floor. Then with a carefully searching fire and with attention to possible moves Hopalong might make, the rifle began to work over the building, first high, then low along the floor.

Hopalong scrambled back farther into the building, frantic for cover, but the shots switched over and back, so that to shift position was not to escape. The building was being literally riddled with rifle fire.

Suddenly he sighted some broken flooring. A dozen or more of the floorboards had been ripped up, leaving a black space below the floor level. Recalling that the foundation of the building was of stone, Hopalong dropped to the floor and lowered himself into the hole. It was shallow, at best no more than nine inches deep, but that was enough. Bullets hit the floor over him, one cut a groove not far from his head, but lying as he did there was less chance of a bullet hitting him—but neither was there any chance of his firing back.

All firing ended as suddenly as it had begun, but there was no move to come near the building. After a long time Hopalong crawled from the hole and made his way carefully to the door. Now all was dark, a ghostly white moon swung lazily above the town, and in the brush a night bird called.

All was still. A board creaked as the night air cooled it, but there was no other sound. Easing from the door, Hopalong retreated toward the bridge, then turned back into the woods and came to his rope by a roundabout route. It still hung there, but he could not see the other end. He glanced at it, his lips dry.

It was three hundred feet to the bottom of jagged rocks. Three hundred feet of emptiness.

He touched his lips with his tongue and, bending over, took the rope in his hands and lowered himself carefully. Then he started out, hand over hand, along the rope. He was not yet to the middle when he heard a light step behind him.

CHAPTER 6

BEN HARDY
COMES CLEAN

For an instant his heart almost stopped beating. The distance below him was three hundred feet and the jagged rocks projected above the water and alongside the shallow stream. To fall was to be killed.

Again he heard the light step, and then smothered laughter—easy, confident laughter that held a gloating note. Carefully he tugged himself along, his hands grasping the rope ahead. He pulled carefully so as to make no more movement than he could help.

If the reata was cut now, he would swing forward against the cliff, his grasp would be torn or knocked loose, and he would fall, his body bounding from one projecting rock to the next in the sheer drop, and then his broken body would hit upon the stones below. No man could live through such a fall. If he did live, it would be to die a lingering death, crippled and broken, on those rocks alongside the stream.

A hand touched the rope, shaking it. Hopalong felt it tremble beneath him. Then it gave a tremendous heave, and he clung desperately. Behind him, on the edge of the cliff, a voice spoke. "A mean way to die, Cassidy. I'd never hoped to find you like this."

So whoever it was knew who he was. But who did? Only his own crowd? No, it had to be somebody else, but over the rush of water echoing against the canyon walls, he could not make out the voice well enough to place it.

Fearing another shake, he swiftly began to pull himself along. The reaction was instantaneous. He felt the line jerk as a knife struck it and slashed through, and then he was falling. He had only time for a quick turn around his fist as the rawhide rope slackened, and then the air roared past his ears and he struck the cliff with a sickening thud, his arms almost wrenched from their sockets. Rocks cascaded from under him and went crashing off down into the stream below. The rawhide cutting into his hand, he clung desperately, unable to lift himself even a little.

There was movement behind him, and then the voice again, louder but as unrecognizable as before. "I don't think you fell, Cassidy, so I'll take no chances!"

A gun roared and a bullet smashed the rock, spitting fragments into his face. Then the gun blasted again and again. The shots picked out spots all around him. Dark as it was, he could not be seen, and as he hung there suspended in the darkness, not daring to move, the unknown rifleman on the rocks behind him continued his careful, searching fire—and Hopalong knew that calculated fire would reach him if he stayed there.

His arm muscles seemed torn from their moorings, and he

could not seem to muster strength to pull himself up. Besides, even if he had, the sound would instantly have indicated his position. Tentatively he reached out a boot toe, feeling for a projection to his right. He found none. He tried with the other foot, and barely touched something to his left. Desperately, while bullets smashed and splintered the rock around and above him, he tried to swing himself enough to grasp a foothold. Dust splashed in his face, then a bullet burned along his side. Another bullet struck the rock within a hair of his fingers, and then he got his toe on that projection of rock, and he held himself there, at least four feet out of the line where he should be hanging.

Finally the drum of shots ended. There was a long period of silence when the unknown man seemed to be listening. Cassidy strained his ears, and could hear the crackle of breaking brush. The man was not pushing his way through the chaparral because the sound wasn't moving very far. It sounded like he was just breaking branches. Why was he collecting dry sticks and leaves?

For a torch.

Sudden fear shot through him! Once it was set aflame, Hopalong would be revealed stark and clear in the glare of light, and then one last easy shot would do the job!

Desperately, his heart pounding, his mouth dry, his hands reached out, feeling the rock wall to his left while still grasping the rawhide rope for life insurance. He stretched, striving to find something that would help him climb. He could be no more than fifteen feet from the rim, but how to get up there? Especially as the rim had, if he remembered right, shelved out a little from the wall.

Then he remembered something. Part of the old abutment was below him! The bridge that led to Sipapu had been built of heavy timber and was of the arch type of construction. The bridge itself had been gone for a long time, but some of the base timbers of the arch remained. Those of the lower part of the arch were set solidly in the rock wall, and these braces had appeared still strong when he had glanced at them from above. Yet how far down were they? Seconds seemed like hours as he thought, trying to imagine the amount of arch needed to bridge that space, and to calculate how far below him that arch might be. To lower himself down the cliff face would be to put him farther from the rim where safety lay. His guns were no solution, for he dared not risk removing a hand from the rope, and in this precarious position he could not turn to shoot.

If his estimation was correct, the arch timbers would be almost directly beneath him, and with great care he began to feel with his toe. He found nothing, and just then a match flared. The man held the match to his bundle of grass, but in that brief light Hopalong saw the bulky timbers below him. He took a deep breath and let go!

Down. He struck and grasped with both arms and found himself gripping the remnants of a big twelve-by-twelve timber that was set on an angle into the rock. Not more than a few feet away was another timber and there were lighter crosspieces. Carefully he pulled his body in behind the heavy timber even as the first of the brush torches fell down the canyon. The flare lit up the canyon like day for a brief instant and showed his rope hanging empty on the wall.

The unknown man was not satisfied. He had evidently

made several torches, for he dropped another almost instantly. It fell, the light flaring upward, but apparently the watcher saw nothing. Hopalong reached back to his hip and released the thong on his six-gun. There was a chance he might shoot the other man, although, backed by trees as he was, his body formed no silhouette, and if he did not get him, he would most certainly give himself away.

He waited, deciding to use the gun only if he was seen. The mysterious man was not yet satisfied. He moved a few steps away and dropped another torch. Evidently he could not see a body upon the rocks below, so decided Hopalong was alive. However, after his fourth drop he must have decided that the body had gone under the water, for he dropped no more.

Bruised and battered, his hand cut by the rope and the other full of slivers from the timber, Hopalong waited. To sleep was to fall. To make a move was to be shot, so he clung to the timber and waited, helpless to do anything to better his situation.

Finally he heard the man leave. Heard the echo of his horse's hooves, and then the long silence that followed. The stars waned at last, and heavy-lidded with sleep, Hopalong dozed slightly. He awakened with a jerk as his hands slipped and he clung there, his heart thudding sickeningly against his ribs. That was close, too close!

He forced himself to remain awake, and at long, long last the sky began to grow gray, and a coolness came down the canyon. Below him the waters rustled and chuckled over their stones. He turned his neck, stiff from its position, and stared downward. Far below was the silver of the stream with deep shadows still covering the rocks.

Hopalong craned his neck back and looked up, and there, no more than twenty feet above him, was the rim. Off to his left, for he now faced the stream and the opposite wall, hung the rope, out of his grasp.

Above, the wall was smooth; below, it was scarcely less so. He was trapped, trapped by his own means of escape, and now he was doomed to die slowly of thirst or exhaustion before anybody could find him.

Painstakingly, Hopalong began searching the cliff face again. Inch by inch he went over it, searching for any crack, any knob, any bulge that might help him. On his left hand the skin was broken and badly cut by the jerk of the rope when he fell, and his right was skinned from the wall and the timber. Despite their condition, he knew the longer he remained where he was, the less his chances of coming out alive.

The Brothers, or one of them, might come to see what the shooting had been about, but otherwise there was small chance of being found by anyone. He was alone here, and if he escaped, he must do it on his own initiative. And escape he must, for aside from his own problem, Topper would be needing water. If he called to the horse, Topper might pull his picket pin and be free, but he might then get it caught in the brush . . . his picket pin . . . *picket rope!*

The instant the idea came to him, Hopalong braced himself, his back to the cliff and his feet on the timber, and pushed himself upward. Balancing, with his feet on the broken top of the old bridge support and his back held as straight as possible, allowed him to reach within eight or nine feet of the rim. He took a deep breath and yelled to the horse. His voice might be lost in the canyon, but he was quite sure he was near enough to the rim to allow Topper to hear him. He yelled again and then again.

He heard the horse quite plainly then, heard him stomping about in the brush. If he could only get loose! If he would come to the edge of the cliff!

Hopalong yelled again and again, and then suddenly he heard a snort and running feet. His eyes riveted on the edge of the cliff, he yelled again. The horse peered over, ears pricked. "I'm in trouble, boy," Hopalong said quietly. "You've got to help me."

The horse looked at the canyon and snorted. He did not like standing on this rim. He did not like the empty space below him, but Hopalong was down there, so it must be all right. Hopalong called to him again. He could see the picket rope trailing back from the bridle, but how to get it over the cliff edge? If he could get hold of that rope, he might make Topper back up and pull him to the edge, and then, if he could get a grasp on the rim, he might get up. He might even be able to cling to the rope and be pulled over. The problem was to get hold of that rope, and from its position it obviously was trailed back between Topper's legs.

"Topper," he said suddenly, "say howdy! Come on, say it! Howdy!"

The white gelding hesitated, then bobbed his head, a trick that Red Connors had taught him as a joke. As he did so, the picket rope came forward a bit. Hopalong stared at it. Although there was now a little slack under Topper's jaw, the rope was still far out of reach. That picket rope was all of twenty feet long, and if it could be gotten over the edge, it would be long enough. How to get it over was the real problem.

Topper was inquisitive and craned his neck, reaching down with his nose toward Hopalong, and although that slid the rope again, it moved it no more than a few inches. If only he had something with which to reach for it!

He stared around him, trying to find something he might use, but the only bush nearby was a bedraggled gray thing that offered little promise.

Where Hopalong now stood was on a brace that had supported the old bridge. This brace was set deep into the solid rock of the cliff and was joined by crosspieces to the adjoining brace. The bridge had been built with an eye toward future loads of machinery and supplies and so had been strongly constructed. He was safe enough where he stood as long as he made no attempt to move around, but there was nothing in the bridge itself that he could utilize for a means of escape.

He looked again at that gnarled and ancient gray bush that grew from the rock near the base of the abutment. Suddenly he dug into his jeans for his pocketknife, and carefully lowering himself to a squatting position, still holding his back against the rock, he cut three of the spreading branches. They were of that tough fiber common to desert woods, and from his belt he took several of the piggin' strings he always carried and lashed the branches one to the other until he had a stick all of nine feet long. To the top he fastened a forked branch with the fork opening downward. Then, careful not to lose balance, he straightened up.

The stick was too limber, but could be managed, and

slowly, carefully, he lifted it up toward Topper. The horse drew back, and Hopalong spoke to him. "Steady, boy! Stand still, Topper!"

As if conscious of what his master planned, the white gelding stood still. The forked stick moved nearer, wavered, then the fork hooked over the picket rope and began to pull it downward, tugging on the loose end of the rope. As it forced a bight over the cliff edge, it became easier, and then, by reaching, Hopalong got his hand on the rope. Carefully he dropped his stick and it fell away into the gorge. Then he wrapped the rope around his body under his arms, tied a bowline so the knot would not tighten too much, and spoke to Topper. "All right, Topper, back up. Back! Easy, now! Back!"

Step by step the white gelding moved back until Hopalong could get his hand on the cliff edge, and then he crawled over. Unsteadily he got to his feet. "Saved my neck, Topper"—he rubbed the gelding's neck and slapped his shoulder—"but it wasn't the first time! Let's go!"

Recovering his rope, Hopalong mounted and turned back through the chaparral, heading for the camp. He had not seen any of the members of his own group since breakfast on the previous morning.

He rode swiftly, and knowing they were headed for home, Topper was eager and kept tugging on the bit, wanting to go faster and still faster. When he appeared from the brush, he heard a yell and saw Pike Towne, rifle in hand, waving to him. The big man came down to meet him, and when he saw the blood on Hopalong's hands and side, he looked up sharply. "What happened to you?" he demanded.

"Long story," Hopalong replied briefly. "Where is every-body?"

"Sarah's here, been keepin' breakfast warm for you. Cindy went off to town, an' Rig took off somewhere before I was up. He was sure you'd had a run-in with some of that Box T outfit. He was fit to be tied."

"I can use some grub," Hopalong admitted, "and about a gallon of water. Tell you all about it while we eat."

Swiftly, as they ate, he told his story, leaving nothing out. He mentioned the Brother he had talked to, and then told of what he had said. As he talked Hopalong noticed that Pike Towne's face grew more and more grim. Suddenly the big man got to his feet and nervously paced about. "Hoppy," he said, "Fan Harlan's in that outfit! Nobody but him ever planned thataway! I'd bet he rode that horse from the stage route to Sipapu, too!"

Watching him, Hopalong nodded. "Could be," he agreed.

"Harlan was always one for that kind of plannin'," Pike continued. "Figured it like clockwork. Fact is, he used to—" His voice broke off as he realized what he was saying, and his eyes swung back to Hopalong. His wife was staring from Pike to Hopalong, her face blank with fear.

Hopalong got to his feet and stretched. "I could sleep for a week," he said, "but I only figure on a couple of hours. That'll rest me up for what we've got ahead of us." He picked up his hat. "How did Shep work out?"

"We doubled our catch." Pike was still keeping his eyes on Hopalong Cassidy, puzzled by his ignoring of Pike's remarks. "But look, I—"

"You know," Hopalong said thoughtfully, holding out his cup for more coffee, "Fan Harlan was alive last we heard. Maybe you're right and he is in this gang."

Pike started to interrupt, but Hopalong continued in a mild voice, "We're sure lucky you'd known him. I reckoned the only man who might know Fan Harlan was dead. You see," he lied, "I heard that Ben Hardy was killed back in the Nation. Even if he isn't dead, he might have reformed, and if a man has reformed, I'd have to judge him according to what he is now, but I'd advise him to keep his name to himself."

Hopalong looked poignantly at Pike Towne, then turned and shook out his bedroll. Towne hesitated, letting out a long breath. He stepped up beside Hopalong. "That isn't all," he said in a choked voice. "Fan Harlan—is Justin Tredway!"

Cassidy examined the old outlaw carefully. "You know this? For a fact?"

"Yes. I saw him in Santa Fe months ago. I thought . . . I thought I was seein' things, but there he was. People told me he was a respected businessman, a retired army officer." Pike took off his hat and ran a shaky hand through his hair. "He used to make up stories all the time, tellin' us about how he'd lived in this place and that. . . . I guess he's still doing it."

"So you followed him down here?" Hopalong asked.

"It took a while to convince Sarah. But I had to know. I had to know what he was up to. I had to know what had happened to Diego and Purdy—and the money." Pike turned away for a moment. "Now we're in it up to our necks"—he looked back and now his old eyes were hard—"and I wouldn't have it any other way. I wish to God Sarah weren't here, but she won't let me send her away, so now we're all in it . . . to whatever the end will be."

Hopalong Cassidy looked long and hard at the man, then shook his head and clapped him on the shoulder. "Well, I'm glad you told me. I'll get that sleep now. You wake me up in two hours. I hope," he added, "that Rig hasn't gone and jumped that Box T outfit by himself!"

Hopalong dropped to his blankets and was asleep as soon as he touched them.

Pike Towne looked over at his wife and their eyes met across the fire. "There," the big man said reverently, "is a man to ride the river with! He's one to tie to!"

Hopalong opened his eyes when Pike touched his shoulders and instantly got out of bed. As he pulled on his boots, his mind was already functioning. Rig was the first thing for even if a holdup was planned, they had no way of knowing its time.

"No sign of Taylor?" he asked quickly.

Pike turned from the fire. "No," he said, "but this came. It was thrown into camp by a stone. Whoever threw it didn't want to be seen and got away very fast. We didn't see it thrown, but it fell right near where Sarah had been workin', so it couldn't have been there more'n a few minutes."

It was a piece of coarse brown wrapping paper and written on it were these words:

TAGGART PAYROLL TO BE STOLEN. HOLDUP GANG TO
HOLE UP IN SIPAPU OVERNIGHT. SHOULD HIT THERE
ABOUT FIVE THIS EVENING. FOUR MEN. IF YOU RIDE
WITHIN THE NEXT COUPLE OF HOURS YOU CAN STOP
THEM AND THERE SHOULD BE A REWARD.

There was no signature. Hopalong studied the writing and
the paper with care, then finally folded the note and put it in his
pocket. "What'd you think?" he inquired, looking up at Pike.

Towne shifted uneasily and drew down his right eyebrow
into a half frown. "We could do it," he said reluctantly. "We could
make Sipapu, an' the two of us might take those boys over. If
we were lucky."

Cassidy agreed. "Well, there's a couple of things about this
that don't look good to me. Whoever wrote this note could have
written it to the mine boss and gotten the reward all for himself.
Or he could have been waiting for these hombres and thrown
down on them. But for some reason he wants us to do it."

Pike's eyes glinted shrewdly. "An' both of us know those
outlaws wouldn't quit. They'd fight."

"And somebody would get killed, maybe a lot of somebod-
ies, including us." Cassidy put down his cup and shucked his
guns, checking their loads as he habitually did before starting
anywhere. "But suppose one member of the gang knew we were
going to show up? Suppose he could fall behind? Then, if they
were wiped out, he would have all the money to himself."

Pike came to his feet. "You mean Fan Harlan cooked this
up? Is that it?"

Hopalong shrugged. "How can we know? But remember,

LOUIS L'AMOUR

the last time the gang was wiped out, he ended with all the money. Why wouldn't he try it again?"

Pike turned and paced the ground. "That skunk!" he said. "That dirty, lyin' . . . " He spun around. "Are we goin' to let this happen?"

Hopalong chuckled and leaned back, smiling a little. "Pike," he said, "we're not going to have to let it happen. It's too late now to stop the actual holdup. We couldn't reach the scene of the crime until after it was over. We aren't going to ride into any shooting match with those outlaws, either.

"Unless we're guessing wrong, Harlan planned this to get the money for himself. That means he has to have it in his possession. It also means that he cannot be with the outlaws when they reach Sipapu. My bet is that he'll take the money himself, cross the Picket Fork at the stage road bridge, and head for home."

"So what is it we're going to do?" Pike asked Hopalong.

Hopalong Cassidy got up and went to his horse. "Figure it out on the way. We won't be in the area in time to do anything if we don't get going!"

Over on Dead Horse Pass, that seasoned old fighter Tom Burnside did not look upon his job as a sinecure. He felt he was on the pass for a serious purpose and he took it seriously. Every day he was in position well before time for the stage and mounted to a platform built high in a tree. From there he sur-

134

veyed the country in every direction through a pair of ancient field glasses.

This platform was known to none but himself, and concealed by the foliage of the tree, it had never been discovered. From this lookout he carefully studied the terrain and every possible place for a holdup. On days when there was no treasure on the stage, he rode around the country, and as a matter of fact, he knew of the old wash as well as Tredway did, recognizing its usefulness to outlaws.

Tredway had visited the place and so had Bill Saxx, and he found their tracks there, although he had no idea to whom they belonged. Sure that he was barking up the right tree, Tom Burnside kept careful watch on the place, and about an hour before time he saw a small party of horsemen come from the bed of the Picket Fork, ride up the bank, and vanish in the direction of the junction of the Picket Fork with Chimney Creek. Burnside was well aware that the old wash ended at the same place, so was not surprised when the riders did not again appear.

Descending from his tree, he rode down the mountain to the foot of the pass, and then down the stage road to the bridge. Turning, he followed up the Picket Fork, and just beyond the intersection of the two streams, he found the mouth of the old wash. Five riders had recently entered there. Convinced of his rightness, he paused to consider his next step.

To ride up the wash would be foolhardy, and he was too wily an old campaigner to do such a thing. It was too late to attempt to ride for help, and he had no right to take any step until a crime was either begun, carried out, or strongly indicated.

If the men donned masks, then he would be free to open fire. Finally, he decided to do the one thing left for him to do. He rode to the Chimney Creek bridge, walked his horse across it so as to make no more noise than necessary, and then he found himself a good spot of concealment in the patch of woods with a good field of fire. He prepared a rest for himself in the crotch of a tree and laid out several cartridges for his long-barreled Sharps .50 buffalo gun. Then he lit his pipe and settled down to wait. He felt good, better than in months. He would show the Taggart outfit they were not wasting money!

Meanwhile Hopalong had arrived at a plan. Unable to prevent the holdup because of the distance, he realized the outlaw gang itself was relatively unimportant. It was the leader he wanted, both for his own purposes and to frustrate his lawbreaking. And that leader would not want to be present when the battle began between the outlaws and the Cassidy outfit.

Pike Towne was to ride at once for the ghost town of Sipapu, and when the outlaws arrived, he was to survey the scene and note all that went on. Cassidy, meanwhile, would try to intersect the trail of anyone leaving the outlaw group. The note could have been sent by any of the outlaws, or by Tredway himself.

They were well on their way to their various destinations before the stage rolled through Dead Horse Pass, thundered across the Picket Fork, raced at top speed across the planks of Chimney Creek bridge, and started through the woods. Tom Burnside got to his feet, knocked out his pipe, and stretched. He was in no hurry. There was plenty of time.

The stage rattled down the road toward the wash, and suddenly riders boiled up as if from the ground. There was a shot, and the messenger rolled from the top of the stage and hit the ground. The driver reached high and at the command from a masked man picked up the reins to restrain the excited horses. "Throw down the box!" The masked man's voice carried through the clear air to where Tom Burnside stood with his empty pipe in his teeth. The old man lifted his Sharps, steadied it in the fork of the tree, and fired!

The heavy .50-caliber slug caught the nearest outlaw right under the shirt pocket, knocking him from the saddle, dead before he struck the ground. Burnside reloaded, and before the amazed outlaws knew what was hitting them, the Sharps bellowed again, and another man dropped. A horse went down at the third shot, and then the outlaws broke into a run.

Forgotten was the heavy box of gold, forgotten was everything but getting out of there. A heavy express packet of bills had already been thrown down, and Saxx had that stuffed into his off saddlebag. Racing their horses, they left the road, circled, and headed for Sipapu.

Vin Carter's face was white as death, but his eyes were bright. "Tipped off!" he yelled at Saxx. "They was tipped off!"

"Tipped off?" Saxx roared back. "It was that durned old buffalo-huntin' ex-deputy, Burnside!"

"Let's rush him!" Pres shouted.

Saxx glared at Pres. "Rush him? You rush him! That old coot would shoot your ears off! He didn't miss anything, did he? Got two men and a horse in three shots, and if that horse hadn't bobbed his head, you'd be dead now. You were lucky to grab that sorrel!"

They raced on away, and Tom Burnside mounted his own horse and rode up to the stage. There he helped load the gold box aboard and removed the masks from the two dead men. Both were Box T hands.

He exchanged a glance with the driver. "Better go on through," he said. "I'll catch up that extry horse and carry these two gents back into Kachina."

"They might come back!" the driver protested.

Burnside's eyes crinkled at the corners. "I don't reckon," he said grimly. "You git along now."

Bill Saxx rode hard for a short distance and then drew up. "Might as well save our horses," he said. "There won't be any pursuit now. Later there will be trouble."

"What'll the boss say?" Pres wondered.

Bill Saxx was thinking of the same thing, and his jaw set hard. "It don't make a durn what he says!" he flared. "Deke an' Windy are back there dead!"

"I'll kill that Burnside," Carter swore, "if it's the last thing I ever do!"

"Lay off him," Saxx warned. "He wasn't foolin' an' he won't be. That old devil's rode with the curly wolves. He's bucked the tiger an' heard the owl hoot. You won't get anything from him but a stomach full of lead!"

Bill Saxx was still stunned by the suddenness of the attack on their rear and he had not reached any definite conclusions about anything. What he wanted more than anything else was to put distance between himself and that stage. That they had shot the messenger, he knew, and that if discovered they would hang, he also knew. Two of their men had been killed and there would have been more had they tried to pick up the bodies. Box T men they were, and it would draw attention to the ranch, but they could always say those men had been fired sometime before.

Suddenly Tredway stepped from the brush ahead of them. His cold eyes went quickly to his foreman's face when he saw that only three horsemen were present instead of five. Yet even as he noticed that he thanked all the powers that be that made him change his mind about going with the outlaws. Actually, he had changed his mind only a few hours before and had promised Saxx to meet him along the way. He had found two logs and dropped them across a narrow gap in the canyon where Chimney Creek cut through a cleft that was almost a tunnel. This allowed him to avoid crossing the bridge after shooting might have drawn the attention of Tom Burnside.

"What happened?" he demanded.

"What's it look like?" Saxx demanded belligerently. "That Burnside was planted down in the trees. He was either tipped off or he spotted us in plenty of time. He drilled the boys right through the hearts. Knocked 'em down like they was tenpins. If we'd stayed longer, we'd have been dead—all of us!"

"You didn't get the gold?" Disappointment was edged in Tredway's voice. Then his keen eyes noted the bulging packet thrust in the saddlebag. "What's that?"

Saxx reluctantly showed the torn corner of the package exposing green sheaves of new bills. "Don't know how much," he said, then added dryly, "We didn't take time to count it."

"We'll carry on then, as planned," Tredway said. "You boys ride on to Sipapu. You've been there since before daylight. You ran into some tracks, one of them looked like a Box T horse, but you were headed for Sipapu to round up stray stock. There used to be some cattle running over there, and as they know we're cleaning the breaks, nobody will be surprised."

Bill Saxx did not like it. He did not like it even a little.

"Suppose somebody has been in Sipapu? How are we goin' to make anybody believe we were there all through the stickup?"

"Nobody will be there!" Tredway said impatiently. "Nobody is ever there! If there is, I don't need to tell you what to do."

"And this money," Saxx inquired skeptically.

"I'll take care of that," Tredway said. "Tomorrow I'll show up in town on the way to get you fellows and see how you've been doing."

Vin Carter stared at the package of money, his eyes ugly. "I don't like it!" he said wickedly. "I reckon we stole that money, so we better keep it!"

Tredway's face hardened and he measured Carter with a careful glance. "And if you're caught with it?" He sneered. "What then?"

When Carter said nothing, Tredway said coolly, "You can see these are new bills. The chances are their numbers are listed. I can handle them by scattering them widely through the East, and I know just how to do it. They'll be watched for only locally. This money is no good to you as it is and is a hanging matter if it is found."

Pres nodded. "He's got somethin' there, Vin. Better listen to him."

"All right." Saxx passed over the money. "But we want to hear from you by tomorrow. If we don't, we're comin' after you. We'll come home on our own."

"If you don't hear from me," Tredway retorted, "I want you to come back to the Box T by all means. You don't think for a minute I'd leave all I've got here, do you?"

Even Vin could see the logic in that, so glumly they watched him turn and stride off through the woods. Once across the logs, he dumped them into the canyon. If they changed their minds now, it would be too late. He was thinking swiftly, and had already decided there was no sense in trying to ambush the lot of them at Sipapu. Instead, he would gamble on Cassidy meeting them there and the resulting casualties. His note should have started Cassidy in that direction. The thing for him to do was to ride at once for the ranch. If anybody came for him, he would be sitting tight, all unaware of any holdup.

He forded the Picket Fork, riding hard, and was heading for the Kachina trail when something happened that pulled him up short.

Far away across the open range he saw a rider on a white horse! And that rider could only be Hopalong Cassidy!

The rider was headed on an angle that would cut his trail to the Box T, and if he rode on, could not miss seeing him, which would ruin his alibi and prove he had been not only off the ranch but in the vicinity of the Picket Fork!

He was still among rolling hills with plenty of cover, but now there was only one way out. He would ride for Kachina. He would come into Kachina from the west. That would do it. He would tell them he had been checking range conditions east of town and had left the ranch but a short time before. That would do it.

Yet as he started for Kachina he was filled suddenly with misgiving. This was not going as planned. It was not going at all as planned. Despite his confidence there was a sudden sinking within him, a growing fear that something had at last gone wrong, and somehow the trouble seemed to build around the presence of one man: Hopalong Cassidy.

CHAPTER 7

WANTED!
HOPALONG CASSIDY

It was dusk when Tredway rode into the main street. A lone hen pecked at some object lying in the street and a few idlers sat on the edge of the boardwalk in front of the blacksmith shop. Tredway rode at once to the livery stable and put up his horse.

"Range west of town is worse than around my home place," he commented to the hostler. "I dislike moving my cattle beyond the place and toward the Picket Fork, but I'm afraid I must."

"They'll get into the brush," the hostler warned, "but I hear you've got some hands workin' up there gettin' cattle out now."

"Yes." Tredway paused, lighting a cigarette. "Some fellows I hired, saddle tramps." He started to turn away, then paused. "You don't know of a couple of good hands I could hire, do you? A couple of mine had to be fired recently. Loafing on the job."

"That right?" The hostler considered a minute. "No, I don't know's I do."

"They were good hands," Tredway added, "until that fellow

145

who calls himself Cameron came around. I contracted with him to get my stock out of the brush, but he and some drifter he has with him strike me as hard cases. These boys of mine have been loafing around up there ever since. I'll have to get rid of that Cameron."

Well satisfied with the planted ideas, he turned and walked on toward the hotel. The hostler picked up his currycomb and turned to the weary horse the Colonel had ridden into town. Now, what did he want to tell me he'd been west of town for? he wondered. That red clay on those hooves never came from anywhere but the ford on the Picket Fork. He cleaned up the horse and gave it a bait of oats, then walked to the barn office and stretched out on the old settee. He was dozing when Tom Burnside rode in with the bodies of the dead men. He did not even awaken when the flurry of excited talk ran up and down the street.

From behind a curtain of his dark room on the second floor of the hotel, Tredway watched the disturbance in the street below. The dead messenger and the two outlaws were unloaded and then more excited talk began as the outlaws were recognized as Box T hands. Tredway stayed in his room, but occasional voices drifted words to him and he could fairly well follow the trend of the talk. There was much excited speculation on how many of the Box T riders had been involved.

He was still standing at the window when the rider on the white horse rode into town.

*　　*　　*

Hopalong Cassidy took care of his own horse, and when Topper was well rubbed down and curried, with hay poked into the manger and oats in the feed box, he turned toward the restaurant. He listened without comment to the excited talk. The fact that the two dead men were Box T riders confirmed his already-arrived-at conclusion.

Evidently the three remaining outlaws had holed up at Sipapu, and would try to regain the Box T on the following day. Pike was smart, and he would take no chances.

Dead tired, he went to the hotel and turned in, unaware of what the next morning would bring.

The hostler had awakened. The red clay on the Colonel's horse did not occur to him as being important, but Tredway's account of the firing of two men did. The news ran through the excited town, and by daylight suspicion had pinned itself solidly on the man Cameron and his partner. The fifth man was generally supposed to be Rig Taylor. The discovery of Hopalong's white horse in the livery barn was the next thing, and at once the town marshal, accompanied by three self-appointed deputies, went to arrest Hopalong at the hotel. They arrived to find an empty room.

When the marshal and his deputies passed his window, heading toward the entrance of the hotel, Hopalong was combing his hair. Their words were plain. "Arrest that hombre right now! Once we get Cameron, we'll ride out an' pick up the others. He was a fool to come right into town after the holdup!"

Hopalong Cassidy's room was on the ground floor, and grabbing up his hat and his rifle, he slid the window up, dropped to the ground, and pulled the window down behind him. Hastily, he ducked down the alley and went around the back of the buildings to the corrals. A woman came to a door to throw out some wash water and she stared suspiciously at him, but he scrambled over the pole corral bars and dropped inside. He walked across, went through a gate and up to the back door of the livery barn. No one was in sight.

Hurriedly, he saddled Topper, cinched him tight, and then spotting a mostly white Appaloosa across the barn, he led that horse over into Topper's stall and tied him there. Then he led Topper out the back door and from the corral gate into a hay field.

Here he was out of sight from anyone except those who might look out of a few windows, and it was no more than fifty yards to the willows along a tiny intermittent stream. Swinging into the saddle, he rode swiftly, circling wide to avoid anyone who might see him; he headed out of town for the Picket Fork.

Cindy Blair ran out to meet him as he neared the wagon. The sun was just over the mountains, although it was past ten o'clock. He swung down from his hard-ridden horse. "Oh, Hoppy!" Cindy rushed up to him. "We've been so worried! Pike's not back and Rig just got in, and we didn't know what had happened!"

"Plenty happened," he admitted. "Where's Rig?"

Taylor was coming toward him, grinning with relief. "What happened to you?" he demanded. "I rode over to the Box T yesterday for a showdown, but there was nobody home."

"Nobody?" Hopalong's eyes sharpened. "How long were you there?"

"How long? Why, I was there all day! There was nobody around but a Chink cook. All the hands gone and Tredway, too. I waited but nobody showed up."

Briefly as possible, Hopalong Cassidy told them what had happened. He told them of the holdup at the dry wash, of the men killed, and that Pike was probably watching the remaining three outlaws at Sipapu right this minute. Then he went on to tell of the events of the night and morning and his flight from town.

"That doesn't make sense!" Rig protested. "Why arrest you?"

"Leave it to Tredway! In the first place, he is obviously not suspected. After all, he is one of the biggest men in town. He wouldn't be slow about realizing that he had to find an excuse for the two Box T men being in the holdup, so what does he do? I can't prove any of this, but I'll bet he claims that they teamed up with us to pull the job!"

"With us?"

"Sure! Look what it would do for Tredway! He'd get you out of his hair, he'd be rid of us and so have the cattle we'd gathered, few as he thinks they are. Also, he would have the guilt saddled on us and would have the money."

"What next?" Rig demanded. "If that's true, there is probably a posse right behind you."

"There probably is," Hopalong admitted. "If they just take a quick look at that white horse, they'll think Topper is still in his stall and that I'm still in town. They won't have any way of knowing just when I left my hotel room. They may waste some time looking around town, but you can bet they'll be coming soon."

"What do we do then?"

"Load up," Hopalong said quickly, "and get the wagon started for Kachina. The women will be safer in town and they can tell their own story there. They can avoid the trail past the Box T, and instead drive east to the old Sipapu trail and go down it until they reach Kachina." He looked quickly at Cindy. "You have money enough to keep the two of you for a few days?"

She nodded, watching him. "Of course. But what then?"

"We'll have time to scout around. Pike may have something we can use. We'll make contact with him, and I've another idea, too."

"What's that?" Rig Taylor asked. "It had better be good. If we go on the dodge, it will look bad."

"How long do you think we'd last in jail in Tredway's town?" Cassidy wanted to know. "My idea is to get in touch with old Burnside. He's no fool. He's been doing some thinking of his own, and believe me, he's too wise in the ways of crooks to be led around by Tredway. If we can get to him with the story, he can nose around some himself, and he'll like doing it."

Within the hour the wagon was rolling, and Cassidy crossed the Picket Fork followed by Rig Taylor. Together they trailed the wagon, but kept out of sight back in the chaparral. Hopalong had no illusions about what was to come. Once in town, the women would be safe, for in the West a good woman was never molested, or almost never. But this would not be the case with

Hopalong and his friends. Tredway would see that the search was relentless, but he alone knew anything of the chaparral, and it was probable that it was much changed since his last venture into the wilderness beyond the Picket Fork.

The covered wagon was almost to the old Kachina-Sipapu trail when Rig suddenly grabbed Hopalong's arm. "Look! There they come!"

A dozen men made up the posse and they came riding swiftly after the slow-moving wagon. In an instant they had surrounded it. Not over seven hundred yards off, Hopalong leveled his strong field glasses at the group and watched. He could make out nothing of what was being said, but he could see the faces plainly enough. Tredway was not among those with the posse, nor was Tom Burnside.

Buck Lewis, the town marshal, was there, and with him were a number of faces Hopalong had seen around town, but none of whom he knew. Cindy Blair stood up in the wagon and appeared to be doing the talking, and apparently she was telling them but good. Hopalong passed the glasses to Rig. "I reckon they'll make out," he said, "but that posse will head back for camp to pick up our tracks."

Rig nodded, then said suddenly, "How about leading them to Sipapu? Maybe they'd run into Bill Saxx."

Hopalong grinned suddenly. "Man, you've got a head on you! Let's do just that! How about that horse of yours? Can he run?"

"He'll run the legs off a coyote!" Rig was grinning. "Let's start 'em!"

Hopalong wheeled to the edge of the chaparral and looked

down toward the horsemen at the wagons. Lifting a hand, he yelled. The horsemen jerked around staring, and he yelled again, then wheeled and let Topper have his head.

The white gelding hit the piñon breaks running like a scared rabbit, with Rig Taylor about a length ahead. They were not far from the crossing of the Picket Fork, and both men knew the exact location of this intersection of the river and the Kachina-Sipapu trail. Riding swiftly, they reached the ford and splashed through, then ran up the trail toward Chimney Creek Canyon. The old bridge was out, but they might at least lead the posse to a place where they could see the abandoned buildings at Sipapu . . . perhaps leading them to investigate.

Riding side by side, the two rode right up to the canyon, then rode off the trail to the right. Almost instantly Hopalong swung at right angles into the dense chaparral, finding a narrow cattle trail. Leading the way, he whipped and turned through it, then spotting a thin place, he lunged Topper at the wall. It gave before him and they pushed through the brush toward the widest and thickest part of the chaparral. This was the section on the east side of the Sipapu trail and an area wherein neither man had worked.

They had been pushing through the brush for some distance when Hopalong suddenly saw the tracks of a rider coming from Chimney Creek. As he correctly surmised, these were tracks made earlier by Tredway when he contacted the outlaws after the stage holdup. He rode swiftly along this trail, keeping out of the tracks so as not to spoil them, and they brought him at once to the narrow portion of the canyon. On the lip there were fragments of bark broken off when the logs had been dropped across the gap. Below, on the rocks at the edge of the stream, they could see the logs.

After a brief glance the two riders turned back into the chaparral. Behind them they could hear the pursuit, but evidently their trail had been lost, for the shouts seemed to be along the creek itself.

Walking his horse, Hopalong led off, found a low bank on the Picket Fork, and forded the stream. Now they were in rolling hills, broken by many deep ravines and much rocky, rough country dotted with cedar and piñon. From time to time they paused to listen, but all pursuit had fallen far behind.

Rig dug out a paper and some tobacco and began building a smoke as he rode. From time to time he glanced at Hopalong, who was studying the terrain with care. "What's on your mind now?" he demanded, his interested eyes watching Cassidy.

"Burnside," Hopalong said briefly. "We're going to pay him a visit."

"And get shot?" Taylor inquired sardonically. "That old coot is nobody to fool with."

Hopalong pulled his hat brim lower and scanned the sunlit hills before him. Slow smoke lifted from among some trees far ahead. That was Tom Burnside's place, but whether that smoke indicated he was at home was another thing. The old lawman was very shrewd in the ways of outlaws and he might be expecting them to try to avenge their comrades. It would not do to take chances.

Rig Taylor began to grow more and more uneasy as they approached. Cassidy kept shifting his advance, keeping to low ground and trees, his eyes alert to every movement, every change in terrain. Finally he drew up. "From here we walk. It's only a little ways now."

Leaving their horses, they started walking carefully along the trail. Although they walked quietly and did not talk, Hopalong made no effort to conceal their passage, knowing that if Burnside caught them sneaking up to his place, he would be inclined to start shooting and ask questions afterward, and he would waste few shots.

Rounding the corner of the barn, they stopped abruptly. Tom Burnside was standing not a dozen paces away. He had a bucket in his left hand and his right was poised to draw.

"Don't, Tom!" Hopalong said sharply. "We're friendly."

"An' you come sneakin' up on a man?" Burnside demanded, his old eyes measuring them coldly.

"Well, we didn't know but what you might have folks here with you who weren't so friendly," Hopalong said.

"Who might they be?"

"Tredway, the marshal, a lot of people right now. They've got us pegged for that holdup today."

Tom Burnside did not speak for a minute. His eyes were shrewd and considering. These men looked like straight shooters, and there was something about that fellow with the gray hair. Suddenly it came to him. "You're Hopalong Cassidy, that Bar-20 gunfighter."

"That's right. I've been going by the name of Cameron up here." Briefly he explained the circumstances. His ride to visit his old friend Pete Melford, the meeting with Cindy and Taylor, and the events that followed. Finally Burnside put down his bucket.

"Let's go inside," he said shortly. "I want to hear more of this."

When he had heard them out, he refilled his pipe without comment, then got up and put the coffeepot on the fire. When he returned to his seat, he said, "Why come to me with this yarn?"

"Because," Hopalong said simply, "you've got more than an ounce of brains, and because you don't go off half-cocked. Above all, you've been a law officer. I figure that with what you've heard from us you can learn a lot more."

"Should be able to," the old man admitted, "an' you bein' who you are means a lot.

"One thing," he said dryly, "seems to have escaped your figurin'. When I was a law officer, only one thing went agin me. It was this outfit you're talkin' about. That Ben Hardy bunch. I'd like nothin' better than to get my hands on 'em."

Hopalong glanced at Rig, then said carefully, "Tom, what would you say if one of those outlaws was alive—I've told you most of them were murdered by Harlan—but living honest?"

Burnside got to his feet and, walking to the door, lighted his pipe. "Don't know," he replied, "but I reckon a man deserves a chance to change his ways. If he was honest, I wouldn't push him. That what you want?"

"This man has worked out an honest life for himself. He's got a wife and he figures on staying that way. It's Ben Hardy."

The old man's eyes glinted. "Hardy, eh? Hardy hisself?" He chuckled. "Why didn't you say so, boy? That Hardy had me dead to rights one time. My horse went down, shot through the head, an' me pinned down. My gun had been throwed from my hand when I fell, an' there I was, cold turkey.

"This Ben Hardy rode up an' stopped. He had a gun in his hand an' I'd been runnin' him mighty hard. He sat there on his horse an' looked down at me, an' he said, 'Now look at you! You're in a deuce of a fix, ain't you?' Then, instead of shootin' me, he put a rope on that horse an' lifted him off me. Then he shook his rope loose an' rode off laughin'!" Burnside chuckled again. "He wasn't a bad lot, that Hardy. I'm sure pleased it wasn't Harlan rode up right then!"

They were silent, considering the situation. Burnside took his pipe from his mouth. "If this hombre is as smart as you figure, he'll have an alibi. He'll say he was at his own place, an' who could deny it?"

"I can." Rig smiled grimly. "I was at the ranch all day."

"Good!" Burnside slammed his fist on the table, making the cups jump. "Is there anybody can back that up?"

"The Chink who cooks for them. He was the only one there."

"That'll help. He might not testify against them, but he'll admit you were there. Anything else?"

"It's a shame we can't prove he got that money from Saxx. If we could find that on them, we might be able to lock them up," Burnside said.

"We'll dig up something," Hopalong told him. "There's some checking we can do. Get a description of Fan Harlan and see how it matches. If we could prove that he and Tredway were one and the same, we could bring him in on any number of charges."

"That would be something." Burnside nodded, his eyes narrowing. "Now, that would really be something."

When Hopalong Cassidy and Rig Taylor moved away from Burnside's ranch, they kept to the brush and timber, riding the hillsides and taking all the precautions to conceal their trail. Mountain and desert men pursued, men trained in the tracking of stock, and wild animals, some of them with the skill of Indians, and they dared leave no smallest hint of their goal or the route they were choosing.

Despite Hopalong's confidence in her, Cindy worried him more than he would admit. The girl was too confident and too daring. Moreover, she was furious at Tredway, who she was sure had stolen the PM Ranch and cattle. As he thought of that the trail grew more rugged and the brush thicker. They turned off the trail and cut across country.

Hopalong led the way and he turned deeper and deeper into the dreaded maze of the pear forest, seeking out trails that led him steadily toward one direction. Rig Taylor rode behind him, his eyes ever straying toward their back trail. From time to time they paused to listen, but heard no sound of pursuit. Hopalong finally turned into an opening that led them to the long-abandoned cabin in the chaparral.

"You figuring on camping here?" Rig asked skeptically. His eyes strayed toward the cabin with its skeletons.

"Tonight," Hopalong replied. "There's water and our horses need rest. No telling when we may have to run for it."

"What then?"

"We'll move on north. Hook up with Pike. Of all the talk I've heard, none of it has been about the country around Brushy Knoll or Chimney Butte. I did hear there was an old trail went that way. I want to see where it goes."

Rig shrugged. "Will the Brothers like that? From all I hear, they consider that their own private preserve."

"No helping it."

Hopalong swung down and stripped the saddle from Topper. After giving him a brisk rubdown with a handful of dried grass, he picketed him and returned to gather wood for a fire. It was no trouble to find dead branches from a couple of fallen trees and some long-uprooted brush. In a short time they had a small fire going and coffee on.

Rig Taylor took off his hat and began to throw a meal together. As he worked he reflected glumly on their situation. From an honest young cowhand headed west to become foreman of a new ranch, he had become an outlaw, pursued by the law. Nevertheless, as he glanced at Hopalong he felt that it was worth it to have such a friend.

Hopalong moved out away from the fire and stood for a long time listening to the night noises of the chaparral. He could hear nothing that he had not expected. No foreign sounds came into this wilderness. A man might as well have stood on another planet, for here he was alone, and if a man were injured in this wilderness, he might never be found, and would die here by himself. And there was little water unless a man knew exactly where to go and how to find it. His eyes lifted over the thick black of the pear forest and looked at the not-too-distant rim of the mesa. No lights showed there, and none on Brushy Knoll. The Brothers were quiet now.

Strange stories had been told of the Penitentes and their mysterious rites, of men crucified in semblance of the Savior, of others whipped until their backs were shredded flesh. This had been true of those in New Mexico, according to report, and these were said to be even more fanatical. There was no telling what might happen up there on Babylon Mesa when the moon was full.

He walked back to the fire with an armful of wood, and the two men ate in silence, listening to the pleasant sound of the water running and the horses cropping grass nearby. Their ears remained attuned to all the noises of the night, and at the slightest change they would have known it at once. There was much to do, but morning would be soon enough to do it.

"We gonna keep watch?" Rig asked. "I'm dead beat."

"Topper will watch for us. If anything comes close, he'll know it before we would anyway. Let's get some rest. We're liable to need it."

Rolled in his blankets, Hopalong watched the stars bright above them and heard the far-off cry of a night bird and the rustling of water, and then he was asleep.

After a long time something stirred in the brush, and Topper looked up, nostrils distended. He listened and rolled his eyes, watching. He did not see the dark-cloaked figure that moved along the edge of the chaparral, then disappeared.

*   *   *

Tredway was sitting tight, but he was worried. The story of the Box T outlaws was going the rounds, and Tredway's story of his firing of the two men and their association with Rig and Cameron was also rumored around. Nevertheless, suspicion would linger among those who disliked him.

The disappearance of Hopalong and Pike helped to increase suspicion against them, and some people now thought Rig was also involved. Yet Tredway was not satisfied. He wanted attention definitely fixed on Cassidy, and he suddenly arrived at a very simple method of attaining his objective. Towne was gone, but money could be planted on Sarah, who lived with Cindy Blair in her wagon in the bottoms.

He had seen Cindy about town and was aware she disliked him, but aside from the possibility that she might be suspected of complicity in the holdup, he had thought of no way to eliminate her. For the first time since the death of Pete Melford, he was worried. His well-laid plans seemed to come to nothing, and despite his efforts he needed money badly. If that fact once became known around Kachina, he doubted whether there would be much loyalty remaining.

Who had sent that note warning him of Cassidy? Sorting over the possibilities, he decided it had to be Tote Brown. That implied that Tote knew who his employer was. Bad as that was, it did simplify things to an extent.

Bitterly he mulled over the situation. He had come a long way in those past years, those hard young years when he had ridden easily and carelessly, confident of his gun skill. In those days he had been proud of his reputation as a killer. By the time he was nineteen, he had slain seven men in gun battles. There had been a few others murdered for their money, a horse, or rifle, and one man killed in his sleep over a petty thing, an argument over a scratched saddle.

All that was in the past, but now the ranch and his wealth were in danger, and all the old viciousness that had lain dormant in his nature returned to the surface. Cassidy, Taylor, and Cindy Blair represented a very definite danger. From the window of the hotel he watched her now as she rode down the street. Anger mounted within him, anger at her coolness, her pride of bearing, her refusal to accept the fact that she was under a cloud.

At that very moment Cindy was thinking the same thing. In the manner of some people she had noticed a certain reserve, but most of them accepted her as she wished to be accepted, and refused to admit that either she or Sarah Towne was at fault. Even the women of the town were friendly, although more reserved than the men. Cindy Blair had the attitude and manners of a lady, and that was enough for them.

Where was Hopalong? Cool as she looked, worry inwardly gnawed at her composure. Out there somewhere were Hoppy, Pike, and especially Rig, who her feelings for, she had come to discover, ran considerably deeper than she ever realized. Right now they might be fighting for their lives, dying in the brush of the pear forest or hiding in some lonely, barren place. There was nothing she could do, and she could not even warn them.

Earlier, she had seen Tote Brown ride out of town, and from talk about the camp she knew who Tote was and what Pike believed of him.

Buck Lewis led his weary posse back into town and they trooped in a dust-covered, straggling line toward the restaurant. He caught the quick gladness in Cindy's eyes as she saw their expressions of disgust and defeat, and he smiled grimly. "Find 'em?" Buck snorted in reply to a question from a bystander. "In that brush? They sent the women to town an' took off. They didn't even leave a trail, no more'n Apaches do. It'll be like lookin' for a coyote on the plains. You know they are there, but you can't see 'em."

Day came at last to the little camp by the water hole, and Hopalong was up and getting the breakfast fire started before Rig rolled out. "You're sure an energetic cuss," Rig commented. "I figured I was an early riser, but you beat me."

"We'll get across the canyon today," Hopalong said, "and we may look around Sipapu a little. Mostly I want to see what we can find up that Chimney Butte trail."

Finally they found a place about six miles above Sipapu where the creek canyon might be bridged, and in a short time, by using an ax they had brought with them from the wagon, they managed to fell logs across the creek from among the bigger trees that grew along the rim. Following that, they built pole rails for each side and led the horses across.

"We'll ride to Sipapu," Hopalong said. "I'd like a talk with Bill Saxx."

They turned their horses down the grass-grown trail and cantered toward the town. As they drew up they detected the slight trail of smoke from the bunkhouse and turned toward it. The men were camped outside and all three looked up in shocked surprise.

Carter reached for his gun, but Saxx dropped a hand to his wrist. "Howdy." The big blond man got carefully to his feet. "Heard you were on the dodge."

"That's funny," Hopalong replied. "I heard you were!"

Saxx studied him without pleasure, not liking the remark or the man. His eyes went beyond Cassidy to Rig Taylor and Pike Towne. The latter had come down from the brush and had fallen in behind Hopalong. Now he moved up beside him, but wide of him. "No visitors," he whispered as he moved past, "but they've been waitin'."

"What do you want here?" Saxx demanded.

"Us?" Hopalong shrugged, looking surprised. "Why, we're rounding up cattle for the Box T. You even visited our camp!"

"I don't mean that!" Saxx snapped impatiently. "What are you doin' over this side of the canyon?"

"Explorin'," Pike Towne said. "We've been seein' lights on that mesa."

"Lights?" Pres didn't like that. He glanced over his shoulder at the dark looming mesa. "Lights up there?"

"Sure. Right above this town. More of 'em over near Brushy Knoll." He looked at them seriously. "You think it's hanted?"

Pres shifted and glanced at Vin Carter, who spat with disgust. "I ain't seen no hants." He sneered. "It's those Brothers . . . the monks."

"Yeah, what do you think they're doin' up there?"

"I don't know, and as long as they don't come down here, I don't care!"

Cassidy dismounted and walked toward them. "How's the coffee?" he asked pleasantly. "Being on the dodge must be rough. I heard the marshal was huntin' you."

"Huntin' us?" Carter demanded angrily. "What would they be huntin' us for? We've got no posse on our trail!"

Bill Saxx narrowed his eyes and stared at Hopalong. Cassidy seemed casual, unconcerned. If he was being pursued, would he act so? Suppose they were being tailed and Tredway knew it but did not tell them. Suppose he was too busy trying to save his own skin.

"Maybe he just wants to ask questions," Hopalong suggested innocently. "Maybe he just wants to know where you were on the day of the holdup."

"If it's any of your business," Saxx replied shortly, "we were on the Box T, right at the house. We left there that night."

Rig Taylor's saddle creaked, but fearing he might speak and give away their knowledge of the foreman's lie, Hopalong said, "Well, then, you've got an alibi. Where was your boss?"

Saxx glared. "You ask a lot of questions!" he snapped. "If you ain't got any business, you better ride on."

Hopalong's blue eyes twinkled over the frost in their

depths. "We might argue that question," he said, "but we won't right now."

As he turned to his horse Pike stepped forward. Looking straight at Saxx, he said, "Ask Tredway whatever became of Ben Hardy, will you? Just to see what he says."

Hopalong grinned as he mounted up. "Well, be sure the marshal doesn't catch you," he said, "or the ghosts."

Bill Saxx watched the three ride off the way they had come, and he scowled. Vin Carter moved up beside him. "I'd like to kill that hombre!" he snarled.

"When you try it," Saxx replied dryly, "be sure you've got an edge. That hombre's gun slick. An' those two with him are not pigeons, neither! That big one, he bothers me. I'm bankin' he's a mean one. Notice his eyes? The way he looks at you?"

"Skeered?" Carter sneered.

Saxx turned sharply around, his gray eyes flat and ugly. "When you ask that question," he said, "you'd better have your hand on your gun!"

Carter drew back warily. "No offense," he said irritably, "but I'm fed up with layin' around. I want action."

"You'll get it, but don't try to tree those boys unless you want to go all the way. They won't run or back down, not that crowd. We'll tangle someday, but when we do, four or five of the six will be dead when it's over. You figure on that, unless"— he smiled—"unless we take a page from Tredway's book an' play it smart."

"You got any ideas?" Carter squinted up at him.

"Yeah," Saxx said, "I got a few. We got to split that bunch up. Take 'em one at a time. Me, I want Cameron."

*   *   *

Hopalong rode swiftly for half a mile, then slowed to listen, but hearing no sounds of pursuit, they continued on. Neither Saxx nor Carter had the balance and cunning of Tredway, and their conversation with Cassidy might stampede them into some hasty and thoughtless action. While such action might give them away, it would be fraught with danger for Hopalong himself and all his friends, particularly for Cindy Blair, at whom they might decide to strike.

Around them the woods grew thicker, and high above them towered the wall of the mesa. Before them, still some distance off, was Brushy Knoll. The air was very still and quiet. Not a breath of wind, not a sound, and there was the smell of dried pine needles, leaves, and hot earth. Hopalong mopped the sweat from his face and dried his hands. His blue eyes were restlessly watching the woods around him and the trail ahead. Despite his common sense, the quiet of the place and the strange stories told of the inhabitants of the mesa worked on his nerves.

"Hoppy." Rig's voice was low and it was worried. "I don't like this! It's too durned quiet!"

"There's no sound but the wind off in the chaparral," Pike agreed, "no sound but the wind."

"Probably," Rig half whispered, "there ain't a soul in miles."

The wind was a low, far-off sound, almost no sound at all, but a background more silent than silence. Rig's eyes shifted to the mesa's rim, then to the trees. He dried his palm on his chap leather and touched his gun.

*   *   *

Two pairs of eyes watched their progress. One pair was high on Brushy Knoll behind an ancient field glass, another was in the chaparral three hundred yards away, and this man held a rifle. Colonel Justin Tredway had succeeded in contacting Tote Brown, and Brown was ready to do his job. His narrow eyes on the trail below, he watched the riders and steadied the rifle in the crotch of a tree.

CHAPTER 8

BABYLON MESA

At the very moment when Hopalong Cassidy talked to Bill Saxx, Sarah Towne was standing at the counter of the general store in Kachina, her face pale and sick. Before her, his hands flat on the counter, was Ira Arnold, the storekeeper. Beside Sarah herself was Buck Lewis, the marshal who had been called back as he was about to leave town. In his hand he held a twenty-dollar bill, a bill that was brand spanking new.

"You're right, Iry," he said dubiously, "this here is sure an unsigned bill, an' as such ain't legal tender, but I don't reckon Missus Towne knowed it or she wouldn't have tried to spend it."

Ira Arnold had never been noted for graciousness. "Ain't necessarily so," he snapped irritably. "Folks try to get away with anything these days, just to keep from payin' their just dues."

Sarah Towne lifted her chin. She looked tired, and now she was frightened. She had found the money in the pocket of Pike's spare pants—had he been implicated in that holdup? The thought had scared her, and while she refused to believe it, there remained a tiny lingering doubt. "Everything I ever bought," she said firmly, "I paid for. I don't owe you anything, do I?"

"No, an' you ain't likely to!" Arnold sniffed. "I know your kind! Traipsin' about the country, no good to nobody!"

"If my Pike was here, you wouldn't say that!" Sarah Towne was suddenly angry.

"That ain't no way to talk, Iry," Lewis interrupted gently. "After all, none of us was born here, an' we'n our folks been movin' for years. That goes for you, too, Iry. Remember I knowed your pa in St. Louis, an' you, too, an' them days neither of you had nothin'."

Arnold glared at him, furious beyond words. Before he could think of anything to say, Lewis turned to the woman. "Where'd you get this bill, ma'am? Ain't no call to be frightened. We here in Kachina don't aim to make trouble for no women."

Ignoring Ira Arnold's sniff of contempt, he continued, "Just tell us where you got it."

"It was in Pike's other pants!" she returned quickly. "And wherever it came from, Marshal, it's honest money!"

"Lady, it's unsigned." Arnold sneered. "Honest money! We all know it came from the stage robbery."

Buck Lewis looked at the storekeeper with ill-concealed irritation. He held his job as a result of selection by a half-dozen men, of whom Ira was one; nevertheless, he disliked the man intensely and admired this quiet, courageous woman in her threadbare garments and with her work-worn hands. She had a quality of courage and an innate fineness that he understood and could appreciate.

"May I see the bill?" Lewis turned at the voice. He knew that voice at once and was relieved. The authority of Colonel Tredway counted for much and far outweighed any opinion held by Ira Arnold.

Lewis handed him the bill, and Tredway glanced at it, then turned it over. "It is unsigned," he commented. "Does anybody have a description of the money taken from the stage? I can imagine no other way in which an unsigned bill could get into circulation."

"What did I tell you?" Arnold was triumphant. "This woman's husband's being hunted right now. He along with that Cameron or whatever his name is. They are a bad lot! Too bad they didn't shoot all of them!"

"I know nothing about it, of course," Tredway said gently, "and without doubt this good woman is innocent of any wrongdoing, but I suggest, Marshal, that you get in touch with the stage company and ask for some information on the nature of the money being shipped. If they were unsigned bills, as now seems logical, this could be a very important clue.

"As I've said, I see no reason for disturbing this woman, but if this money came from her husband's trousers, then no doubt our suspicions are correct and he is one of the outlaws we seek."

"I'll check on that," Lewis agreed, "right away."

Sarah Towne glanced once toward the piled-up groceries, then turned away from the counter, her heart beating rapidly. Something was wrong about this, very wrong! Pike had promised her and he couldn't have . . . Or could he? Then she shook her head decidedly. Pike might have been many things, but he was a man of his word, and furthermore, he loved her too much. Nothing would ever shake her faith in that love.

Colonel Tredway's face was grave, but inwardly he was glowing. Nothing could have worked out better! Not only was suspicion thrown right where he wanted it thrown, but he had appeared as a friendly witness and would never be suspected of having planted that bill himself. This was one more step in the elimination of the Cassidy-Taylor-Towne combination, and with them out of the way, he was safe.

That the bills had been unsigned he discovered upon opening the package. That did not trouble him, for among other things he was a skilled penman, and upon occasion could do a good job of forging. Also, he smiled slightly, this would keep the money in his hands and keep him in control of the situation.

Sarah Towne returned to the wagon to find Cindy Blair had returned from her ride. Quickly she told her story.

"It's absurd!" Cindy flared. "Something is wrong! They had no chance to rob any stage even if they had been the kind to do it! I'm going to see Marshal Lewis!"

On second thought she changed her mind. It would do no good to go to him and lodge a protest, none at all. Before they could do that, they must have evidence.

"If they didn't have that money, and we know they didn't, then how could it have been there for you to find?" she asked, speaking more to herself than to Sarah Towne. "There's only one answer. Somebody had to put it there!"

She started for the wagon. "Sarah, show me where those pants were hanging."

Sarah pointed at the hand-carved wooden hook inside the covered wagon. Inside, but within easy reach of a man who got up on the back of the wagon. Getting down, she looked carefully around. Their own footprints were all over everything. Despairing of finding anything, she nevertheless began to scout around. Her eyes suddenly fell on a pair of boots, and looking up, she saw a quizzical pair of gray eyes looking from a seamed brown face. The man was old, but stalwart and strong, and his mustache was white except for a slight yellowing from tobacco stains.

"Huntin' somethin', ma'am?"

She hesitated, uncertain whether to be friendly or not, but the old man looked pleasant enough. "I'm hunting some tracks," she said then, and went on to repeat the story of the morning's happenings. He watched her as she talked and glanced from time to time at Sarah Towne, who had joined them.

"My name's Tom Burnside," he said quietly. "I used to be some shakes at trackin'. Suppose you let me have the job?"

Turning away from them, he began a careful examination of the ground, swinging in a slowly widening circle about the area in which the wagon stood. Suddenly he knelt, examining a sharply delineated track.

It was the print of a new boot, the toe pointing toward the wagon, part of it obliterated by grass on which the walker had stepped, part in soft loam. But the overall impression was excellent, better than he had hoped for.

Two hours of careful work took him back to the rocks at the edge of the little stream that flowed by the town. On those rocks the walker might have come from anywhere, gone to anywhere. You had only to come out of the back door of one whole side of the town and walk down to the stream. The worn boulders held no mark of any kind. Yet he was impressed by what he had found. Without doubt somebody had circled around and crept up close to the wagons. That somebody might have planted the bills. It was then he made up his mind to go to Buck Lewis.

On the trail near Brushy Knoll, Tote Brown suddenly had Hopalong Cassidy in his sights. He disliked firing on one man when there were others with him, but his orders were explicit and the price better than usual. He squeezed off his shot.

No one has ever recorded the place of little things in the chain of history. On this occasion it was a big horsefly that buzzed near Topper's ear, and Topper shied slightly. Something stung Hopalong sharply across the top of the ear, and the sharp report of a rifle rang out, echoing against the face of the cliff.

Racing their horses for the trees, Hopalong put one hand to his ear and it came away bloody. He stared at his fingers, then looked at Rig with disgust. "A half inch closer and that would have blown the top of my head off!"

Too wise to start charging up the side of the tree-covered slope that lay below the precipice, the three waited and listened, but there was no sound. "Now, who d'you suppose fired that? One of those Brothers?"

Cassidy shook his head. "What about that hombre who shot at you, Rig? It could be the same one."

"Where does he fit into this?" Taylor demanded. "I don't get it."

"If my guess is right, he's working for Tredway. He may have been trying to keep you from discovering Pete Melford's place, but now I guess he's after all of us."

"Either of you want to go back there in the brush after him?" Hopalong touched his bloody ear and looked from one to the other, grinning. "Well, neither do I. Let's Injun out of here and push on."

Tote Brown had retreated from his position but only to a better one selected earlier. He had hit Cassidy; even if the bullet had not killed him, it had hit him. He had seen that much. Now, if they came after him, he could get one of them and maybe all. From his present position they could not see him, and to get at him they must dismount and come up the slope toward him. His own horse was across a narrow gap and beyond a rocky area that could not be crossed by a horse. His chances of getting one man and maybe more were excellent, and his own chance of being hit was slight.

He waited and waited, but nothing happened. Were they lying below him, watching from under cover? He dared not approach the trail now. He must wait or retreat. He swore softly. It had been too much to expect, of course. But if they had come! His eyes gleamed with malice and he got to his feet, but as he straightened up and turned a queer feeling came over him, a feeling of being watched. His rifle at the ready, he looked around very carefully, then started down the rocks in the direction of his horse.

Suddenly there was a rustling in the brush ahead of him. Frozen in place, he listened. Behind him a twig snapped. He peered through the leaves but could see nothing. He thought he could feel the weight of unseen eyes upon him. He took a long slow breath and stepped forward. He sensed movement all around him, just out of sight, on the lowest threshold of his hearing. . . . A shadow shifted on his left, a whispering in the branches to his right. Behind him . . . He whirled for an instant and saw . . . A cloak? A hooded figure in the trees?

Tote Brown was not, or he had never considered himself, a superstitious man, yet all around him the brush seemed to have come to life. He had heard of ghosts around Sipapu and had sneered at such stories. He had heard bizarre tales about the inhabitants of Babylon Mesa, but he had believed none of them. He stood frozen, looking around and trying to locate the origin of the movement, but he could find nothing. All was very still, and there was no other sound.

After a while he started on, and he walked softly, as if fearful of attracting attention. Was he going crazy? Or was his imagination playing tricks on him? As he neared the place where his horse had been left, he began to hurry. Rounding the last clump of rocks and brush, he was almost running. He slid to a halt, staring, wild-eyed, suddenly frightened. His horse was not there!

Dragged its picket pin? Hurrying forward, Tote looked at the ground. He could track the . . . There were no tracks. There was no evidence that a horse had ever been here.

It was the wrong place, that was it! He hurried on, but an hour of searching brought him nothing. Panting, he stopped and mopped the sweat from his brow. Gone! They had taken his horse, then. But who were they? What were they?

He was thirsty and wanted a drink. He should never have left his canteen on his horse. Thinking swiftly, he made up his mind. There was no use looking further. He would start for Chimney Creek. By keeping the cliff at his back, he could go right to the stream, and it could not be far off. Yet even as he started to retrace his steps he began remembering that cliff. Nowhere in all the length of the canyon he had examined had he seen where a man might get to the bottom!

But there would be a way. There had to be a way.

In a flash it came to him. The place to go would be Sipapu! Why had he not considered that? Bill Saxx would be there with his men and he could give them some cock-and-bull story about being thrown. It would be simple enough. He started off, walking rapidly. It might be four or five miles. It could not be more than that.

The region between Chimney Creek Canyon and the mesa was not a dense thicket of brush but rather scattered clumps of trees, thick groves of aspen, and much grass. He walked rapidly, but the heavy rifle began to tire him. Finally he made a sling with a strip of rawhide and hung it over his shoulders. He could carry it more easily then, but it gouged into his back from time to time, and he kept shifting it as he walked.

It was very hot. His mouth felt dry and his brow was fevered. He touched his tongue to his lips and walked on. The clumps of trees kept him walking around them, and several times he had to stop and correct himself, for he was walking out of his course. His face felt hot, but he slowed now to conserve energy. Dusk was nearing when at last he sighted the town. Barely able to restrain himself from running, he hurried toward the place. Earlier, as he followed Hopalong and his friends, he had seen Saxx there, and so he went at once to the camp.

It was deserted and still. The ashes of the fire were cold. They were gone—gone!

But there was water—there had to be water! Yet a hurried search netted him none. The well that had once supplied the town was caved in. A trip to the creek found him standing on the old abutment of the bridge, but below him it was a sheer drop of hundreds of feet down to the water.

Slowly he got to his feet. How far it was to a place where he could descend to the river he did not know. Nor did he know in which direction to start. Frightened, he took what seemed the best chance and started downstream. He no longer even thought of his missing horse. His problem now was water, and he knew of no nearer chance to get water than the bridge on the stage road.

It was very hot. He slowed his pace and shifted the heavy rifle. Suddenly he realized for the first time that he might not get out of this alive. He started to walk again. Once he stumbled, and a dozen yards farther he stumbled again. He would have to take his time, he would have to be careful of his strength.

Hopalong Cassidy rode in silence, considering the situation. The thing to do, he realized now more than ever, was to see the Brothers. They might actually know something, and they might give evidence. And now was the time to find out. That there was a trail to the top of the mesa in the vicinity of Brushy Knoll had long been rumored. The one Brother he had talked to knew of Pete Melford and he was hoping to enlist their aid in proving the guilt of Tredway and establishing Cindy Blair's claim to the PM range.

"Look," Pike suggested suddenly. "I'm worried about Sary. If you don't think you'll need me, I'll head back for town. I want to be sure they are all right."

Hopalong drew up. "No, I won't need you, and it would be better if I went alone. Rig, you might as well go with him unless you want to come along. He may need help, and I surely won't. Also," he added, "you will be headed back where that shot came from, and two can watch out better than one."

"You sure?" Rig asked. "I'd sure like to see atop that mesa, but I'm worried, like Pike is. No telling what may happen with the womenfolks by themselves."

"See you then!" Hopalong turned Topper back into the trail. "No gunplay if you can avoid it, but watch out for Saxx. He's bad."

After they had started back, Hopalong pushed on down the

old trail. It showed no evidence of recent use. The only tracks he saw were those of deer or smaller game. At his right the wall of the mesa loomed high, and already the hour was growing late and it was nearing dusk. Several times he cast curious looks at Brushy Knoll, but it loomed up, dark and ominous, with the shadows gathering under the leaves of trees and brush, and gave no sign of light or life.

The trail branched suddenly, and here he dismounted and examined the dusty earth carefully. There were tracks here, tracks of men wearing sandals. The trail they had taken was that leading from Brushy Knoll to the mesa, and the latter wound by a switchback route up the steep rock wall. Hopalong glanced up at the wall and could dimly see the line of the path. "Let's try it, Topper," he whispered. "You're a good mountain horse."

Topper moved willingly into the path, his ears pricked forward inquiringly. There was no sound but the creak of the saddle leather and the soft thud of Topper's hooves in the dust of the trail. Long twilight shadows fell across his path and trees loomed on both sides. Once Hopalong half believed he glimpsed someone or something moving far back in the brush, but the movement faded and he rode on. And then the trail started up the slope.

It was just wide enough for a man on a horse and it was bare rock. Topper started up the trail, a slight incline that became steeper, then rounded an elbow and started back. Slowly they mounted, and when Hopalong looked out over the wide country below them, he could see the vast miles of the chaparral and pear, stretching away in every direction from the foot of Babylon Mesa.

Then, at last, he rode out in the clear, high air of Babylon Mesa. Immediately before him the mesa was flat and grass-covered. Hopalong spotted several head of cattle who looked up curiously.

Beyond the grassy level was the darkness of a pine forest, and Hopalong rode toward it. Topper walked steadily. Something moved along the edge of the pines on his left. Without changing pace, Hopalong let his eyes shift along the front of the trees and saw another movement on his right. They knew he was here, then. And they were letting him come.

The stars came out and hung so close overhead in the clear air that it looked as if they could be knocked down with a stick. The path entered the forest and he moved on, and then suddenly men closed in from the right and the left. Not one man, but a dozen. They walked, six men to a side, and they said nothing, nothing at all.

Suddenly the trail turned; a man was standing there with a lantern. He was a big man and he wore a beard. He said nothing, but stepped into the path ahead of Hopalong. They emerged from the trees and Hopalong could see the dark lines of row crops, acres of them, he could see lights glowing from the windows of low adobe structures, and somewhere he heard a woman singing.

There was the smell of damp earth, and in one of the fields he saw water between the rows. So they irrigated. A good water supply, then. It would not be suspected above this wall of rock.

The guide with the lantern paused before an open door and

one of the men moved up to Hopalong's stirrup. "You may get down," he said.

Hopalong Cassidy swung down and stripped off his gloves, tucking them into his belt. He smelled the rich sweetness of honeysuckle. They walked down a path and through the door. Within the room all was light, and three men sat behind a table on a raised dais at the end. Arranged along the walls on benches were two dozen other men. Most of them were bearded. All were dressed in rough homespun robes of some sort.

The man in the center behind the table had a gray beard, but he was a man still strong and of massive build. He looked down at Hopalong. "Why do you come to this place?"

Briefly Hopalong Cassidy explained, beginning with his arrival to see his friend, the shot Tote Brown fired at Taylor, the discovery that Taylor and Cindy Blair had come to claim the ranch left by his friend. He told them briefly and concisely all he knew, and then he stated his reason for coming.

"It has been said that you keep watch from this mesa," he said. "It seemed to me that some of you might have seen something related to the robbery that might help us. If this is the case, it would be necessary that whoever saw it happen come down and testify in court."

The elder listened, then shook his head. "That we cannot do. We have committed ourselves to a good life. We take no part in the disputes or altercations of those who live around us. We do keep such a lookout as you describe, but only to preserve our own peace.

"Here"—he gestured around him—"we have all we need. Indeed, from observation, we know that we live much better than most of those on the ranches below. We have sheep, goats, and cattle. We have vegetables, grain, and fruit. We raise what we need and we use what we raise, and we keep a granary supplied against the bad years. We have no need to traffic with others."

"Nevertheless," Hopalong replied, "you are men of justice. Would you see a relative of Pete Melford robbed, a girl who has done no harm to any man?"

"We know, of course, that the PM range was settled by Melford. We do not know what happened after his death, and even had we suspected anything was wrong, it still would not have been our place to interfere. We handle our own affairs, dispense our own justice, our own punishments."

"The man we know as Colonel Justin Tredway," Hopalong said, "came to this country after the breaking up of the Ben Hardy gang. We know now that most of that gang were killed down in the chaparral. Ben Hardy escaped, and Fan Harlan was the killer. Justin Tredway has been positively identified as Fan Harlan."

The elder's head came up sharply, and Hopalong heard a mutter of startled sound run through the room. The three men behind the table bent their heads together and talked in low whispers. There was much talk in undertones among the others. "You have reasons for what you have said? Explain, please."

Hopalong repeated his suspicions to them, adding what he had learned from Pike and from Burnside. The atmosphere of the room underwent a change as he spoke. They questioned him at length about the finding of the skeletons of the outlaws, then about events in Kachina surrounding their arrival and events concerning the Box T. They asked many questions about Tredway and Saxx and seemed interested in Tote Brown. They asked questions about the physical description of the men, their actions and background. Particularly they asked about the opening of Kachina, the beginning of the freight line, and then more about Tredway.

Finally Hopalong arose to go, and the elder leaned over the table. "We may be able to help you," he said, "and we will do what we can. We can send a man who will testify to the fact that Melford lived on and developed what was known as the PM Ranch. Beyond that we can make no promises."

The guide with the lantern appeared once more and led Hopalong to the trail, this time escorting him all the way to the bottom of the cliff. "I have been requested," he said, at the foot of the trail, "to ask you to say nothing of what you have seen. We do not welcome visitors."

A few miles away from the trail Hopalong turned into the brush and made a dry camp, more than a little mystified by what he had heard. What was it about Tredway that interested them so much? For despite the fact that they had been careful to ask seemingly casual questions, he was the one subject to which they continually returned.

Twice during the night he awakened, and each time there were lights on Brushy Knoll that could have been nothing but signals—to whom?

*   *   *

Evenas watched the last guest climb the stairs to his room in the hotel. His mind was made up. His statement to Hopalong that he would be wealthy, and soon, would wait no longer for results. Tonight was the night.

Glancing around, he dropped to his knees in front of his hiding place, then hesitated. No, better not. Tonight he would make his play, but he would make it on nerve and the knowledge of what he possessed. Removing his green eyeshade and placing it on the desk behind the counter, he took from a drawer a double-barrel derringer and thrust it into his coat pocket.

He stepped outside and the wind whipped his coat, and he dropped his head and walked around the hotel toward the stable. As he saddled his horse he felt his first moments of doubt. The Colonel could be hard as nails—his whole past proved it—and any man who bucked him would be asking for trouble. Yet did Tredway dare take a chance now? Cassidy was around, and Cindy Blair.

If Tredway was the man he thought him, he was fast with a gun, and he might not hesitate to shoot. Evenas knew he could not hope to compete with any slightly handy gunman, so he hit upon a clever scheme. In the lobby of the hotel he had picked up an old newspaper and rolled it carefully. Then he cut a hole in the side of the flattened tube for his finger. Unrolling the paper, he inserted the derringer in the center of it and rolled it once more. Now he could carry the innocent newspaper in his hand while his finger would be on the trigger at all times.

Despite his precautions, much of his confidence began to ebb away. Memories of the stern jawline of Tredway and his harshness returned. And Evenas had no illusions. He was not a brave man.

The road at that hour was deserted and he saw no one. He rode at a canter, his head bowed against a stiff wind. The lights of the Box T appeared and he stared at them, holding his hat to his head with one hand. Lights in the bunkhouse, too. He had hoped the hands would be away from the ranch. Yet, as he watched, the lights in the bunkhouse dimmed and went out, a man walked to the barn, mounted a horse, and rode swiftly away.

Evenas stared at the lights in the house, his mouth dry. This was it. For more than a year he had been building toward this moment. One swift reach for wealth, then escape and the freedom to enjoy it. He would need all his nerve to face Tredway. Setting his jaw, he started forward, the newspaper clutched in his right hand, his finger on the trigger of the gun. He had promised himself wealth and the time had come to make good that promise. He started his horse down the hill, watching the ranch house with no goodwill. He dismounted and tied his horse to the hitch rail, then went up to the door. He hesitated briefly, his hand lifted to knock. Through the lighted window he could see Tredway seated at his desk, writing. Evenas waited for a lull in the wind, then dropped his hand to the knob and tried it gently. Slowly it opened under his hand and he stepped in, away from the sound of the wind.

His boots made no sound on the beautifully woven Navajo rug as he crossed the hall to the study door. He paused in the open doorway. Warned by the sense of some presence, Tredway looked up.

For an instant he was startled, and then he recognized the sallow-faced, black-eyed clerk. "What do you want here? Who let you in?"

"I walked in. I thought you wouldn't want to be disturbed." Evenas stared at the quiet-faced man sitting before him. It was a strong, authoritative face, and only a closer look would bring out the tiny lines of acquisitiveness about the eyes or show the cruel mouth below the mustache. Hate mounted within Evenas, hate for this crisp, sure man who sat there at the table. Tredway was a thief and a murderer, yet he sat there so calm, so sure of himself!

Well, he would destroy that calm. From now on he, Evenas, would be boss. The feeling filled him with triumph. He took a step into the room, the rolled-up paper in his right hand. "Tredway," he said, "I want five thousand dollars tonight and twenty thousand before the week is out."

Tredway's eyes narrowed. Ever since he had realized the identity of his visitor, he had been puzzled. He knew the man, knew him for a sneak who if not watched would filch coins from the till, who would even steal small things from the rooms. He had never suspected that the man might try blackmail. A momentary smile touched his lips. It was an ironic smile, for Tredway was thinking that aside from the stolen, unsigned bills, he had less than three hundred dollars on the place.

The smile disconcerted Evenas and made him angry. The newspaper lifted slightly, and for the first time Tredway's eyes went to that paper. Instantly he realized his danger. Evenas was a growing kitten playing with an old alley tomcat. Tredway no sooner noticed the paper than he realized that no man would have carried a paper in his hand through all that wind outside. Therefore the paper was either some evidence with which Evenas planned to confront him or it concealed a weapon. Tredway had ridden with the wolves too long to be deceived.

"I mean it!" Evenas's hatred made him bold. He stepped farther into the room. "I didn't come out here to talk! I want five thousand dollars and I want it now!"

"You've neglected to tell me," Tredway said smoothly, his cold eyes never leaving those of Evenas, "what I'm supposed to get for the five thousand, or why I should give it to you. Is this a shakedown?"

"Call it whatever you like." Evenas sneered a little. "I know who you are. I know about Melford and the PM. I know enough to hang you. I don't care what you've done, all I want is money."

"I see." Tredway studied Evenas with contempt. The petty fool! Did he think he could get away with this? That the man should even carry such an idea angered Tredway. "And for that money, what do I get?"

Evenas shrugged. "I won't go to Lewis with what I know. Nor to Hopalong Cassidy."

Tredway's eyes flickered a little at that name. "So you know him, do you?"

"The whole town knows who he is," Evenas replied shortly, "but I'm the only one who knows who Pike Towne is."

"Pike Towne?" The name was unfamiliar, and his puzzlement was plain in his face. It increased Evenas's certainty. If this man did not even know who worked for him—

"Pike Towne is the fellow who's been helping Cassidy work your cattle out of the brush. He and Rig Taylor."

"You say you know who he is? What of it? He means nothing to me." Tredway was talking and watching to get Evenas off guard. He had known for several minutes that he was going to kill him, but not at once. He wanted Evenas to see the folly of his actions, he wanted him to regret his temerity in coming here. And then he could die.

"That's what you think!" Evenas sneered. "Pike Towne is Ben Hardy!"

"What?" Tredway's eyes bulged. "You're crazy! Ben Hardy was killed in—" Then he realized what a complete giveaway his action had been, and he sagged back in the chair, taking the precaution of letting his hand fall to the gun that rested in a holster fastened to the underside of the desk.

"No, he isn't dead." Evenas leaned forward across the desk. "He isn't dead. That's Ben Hardy out there, and he knows who you are. What do you think he'll have to say to you?"

Tredway's face was impassive, but behind it his brain was working desperately, not upon the situation that faced him, but upon the threat implied by the presence of Hardy. Suddenly he no longer doubted that it was Ben, and he remembered that while he had always held the other man in contempt, he had always been a little afraid of him. There was no fooling about Ben, and if he was back here, it must be for a reason. And working with Cassidy! What did that mean?

"Come on, Colonel," Evenas urged, "I want my money. I've got evidence hid out that will be all Cassidy or Marshal Lewis would need, to say nothing of Hardy."

Sure of his success now, Evenas was wondering why he had ever been afraid of this man. That was the way of it; they looked tough and sounded tough, but they were soft enough when you faced them.

"All right," Tredway said, "but I've not anything like five thousand out here. Didn't you ever think of that?"

To tell the truth, Evenas had never considered it, and suddenly he was cursing himself for a fool. Out here he had been sure he could talk without being disturbed, but if Tredway had no money here, why—

"I'll have to go to town to get that much," Tredway said quietly. "Five thousand is a lot of money, and I never keep over five hundred on the place."

Now, a ride through the darkness and wind to Kachina was the last thing Evenas wanted to undertake, not with this man at his side or even ahead of him. There was too much chance of losing him in the darkness, and after that there was no telling what Tredway might do. Despite his growing contempt, an underlying sense of reason prevented Evenas from making a complete fool of himself.

Regretfully he made his choice. "Give me the five hundred you say you have here," he said, "and a check for the remainder. You can tell them at the bank I'm doing some buying for you, and you can write me an authorization to ensure my getting the money." He smiled. "That will do it."

"All right." Tredway started to move, his hands resting on the table to push himself erect. As he reached his feet his right hand swiftly scooped up the coal-oil lamp and smashed it at Evenas. The lamp chimney shattered and the bowl of the lamp, catching the corner of the bookcase, broke. Oil splashed over Evenas's hands and coat, and some of it struck his face and eyes.

Blinded, he sprang back, dropping the derringer wrapped in the paper and pawing at his eyes. Fire flashed in the oil and his coat blazed up. Screaming, he sprang back, and Tredway calmly stepped behind him and smashed the barrel of a gun over his skull. As the clerk dropped, Tredway scooped up an Indian rug from a chair and threw it over the clerk's body, smothering the flames.

He walked into the next room and lit a lamp. He brought it back and placed it on the desk. Pocketing the derringer, he went through the unconscious man's pockets, then grabbed his coat collar and dragged him outside.

Saddling his own horse, Tredway walked back to the clerk, who was just beginning to stir. Brutally he kicked him in the ribs. "You weak-kneed fool!" he said contemptuously. "Whatever made you think you could get away with this?"

Moaning in pain from his burned hands and face, Evenas struggled to get up. Tredway kicked him again, then helped him erect. "Get on your horse!" he said violently. "Hurry it up!"

"I can't!" Evenas cried. "I'm burned! Get me a doctor!"

Tredway shoved him. "Get up in that saddle or I'll kill you!" he said. "I want those papers and I want them now! Understand me?" His lips thinned down. "You don't get a doctor until I get those papers! Now get started!"

Blindly Evenas crawled into the saddle. Pain seared his face and his hands were raw. All thought of money was gone. All he wanted was to escape the pain, the awful pain.

CHAPTER 9

BLACKMAILER'S CACHE

Hopalong Cassidy rode through the woods toward their old camp on the Picket Fork. For some distance he had been aware of the utter silence around him, and yet it was not until he came within sight of the corral that he understood why. The cattle were gone!

Riding forward at a lope, he swung down and studied the ground. Near the gate and close to the corral fence he found a boot print. Mounting up, he swung into the trail of the cattle and soon realized that the herd had been driven off by at least four riders. They were headed straight across country toward the Box T.

Tredway had wasted no time in claiming the cattle. Had he by some chance discovered the larger herd hidden in the chaparral? From the size of this herd, Cassidy doubted it. There was no time now to look and see. He would follow this herd until he was sure it was proceeding toward the Box T, and then he would ride to Kachina. It was time for a showdown.

Topper was in fine fettle. The white gelding had always been a horse that loved to travel, and all he needed to recoup his strength was a few hours of rest, water, and a little feed. He was tugging impatiently at the bit, wanting to go.

Hopalong removed his bone-handled guns from their black holsters and wiped them carefully, checking the loads as he always did. Then, returning the guns to their holsters, he pushed on, squinting his eyes toward the far-off smoke of Kachina and then back toward the parched range. There was no dust column and everything indicated the cattle had been moved on the previous day. Yet there was little chance they would be taken beyond the Box T itself. There had been something more than three hundred head in that corral by final count, while in the inner corral there were many more.

Turning off the Box T trail, Hopalong started toward Kachina. He was under no illusions about what faced him. Tredway had not gotten where he was, outlaw or not, without being a man of ability. He would not be defeated by any simple means, or without a fight.

He was turning from the trees near the trail and no more than a mile from town when a sorrel horse raced across the road and headed him off. It was Cindy Blair. "Don't go into town, Hoppy! They are going to arrest you!"

"What do you mean?" Hopalong demanded, catching her bridle. "For the stagecoach robbery?"

"And murder! They already have Rig and Pike! They arrested Pike for possession of stolen money, and they arrested Rig for the killing of Evenas!"

For an instant the name Evenas meant nothing to him, and then he recalled the sign on the hotel desk. "The hotel clerk?"

"Nobody knows what happened. They found him on the trail this morning, his face, hands, and coat burned, and he had been shot three times in the back."

"Evenas?" Hopalong scowled. "Where did he fit in?"

"I don't know. Rig was scouting around town. He'd heard they were moving our cattle, and he was seen near where the body was found."

"Did he see anybody?"

"I haven't talked with him. He's in jail and I just found out about it. Pike got word to me through Sarah, and I was to stop you before you were arrested, too. It looks," she added bitterly, "like Tredway is trying to get rid of all of us!"

Briefly she recounted all that had taken place, including the finding of the money and the trouble at the store. "We told Tom Burnside," she concluded, "or, rather, I did."

"You couldn't have done a better thing." Hopalong considered the situation. Tredway had the cattle and there was no way they could protest without being picked up by the law, and if they were picked up, Tredway was sure to see there was evidence enough to get convictions. He was cunning, and he knew this country. Above all, many of the people in Kachina were dependent on him for their livelihood.

Whatever was to be done would have to be done fast. Burnside might discover something, but they could not afford to wait on that.

"Go back into town," he said, "and file a claim against those cattle that Tredway drove off. Get Buck Lewis to block any sale of them until this matter is settled."

"I can do that, I think," she agreed, "but what then? Rig and Pike are in jail."

"I've a hunch," he said, "but I'd better get busy on it." He had suddenly recalled the details of his conversation with Evenas. The comment that he had made—that he had wealth at hand. And he had just been talking of Tredway. It might mean nothing at all, but it was curious the way the man had turned and dropped to his knees on the floor as Hopalong left. Suppose there was something concealed there that in some way affected Tredway?

Suppose—and he realized he had nothing on which to rely as evidence—that Evenas had discovered something about Tredway and had attempted blackmail? Had Tredway managed to get the hiding place from Evenas? If there was any evidence and if there was a hiding place.

Circling the town, Hopalong dismounted and picketed Topper well back in a nest of trees. There were other horses close by and the grass was good, so there was no chance that he would be hungry or restless. Watching from the edge of town, Hopalong took a chance and moved into an abandoned building. From within it he studied the street.

Buck Lewis came out of the Elk Horn and walked up to the Mansion House, then on to his office. He had paused briefly before the Mansion House, talking with someone on the porch. A moment later Hopalong saw Tredway come down the steps and walk toward the Elk Horn.

Then Cindy Blair appeared, riding her sorrel. She rode up

to the marshal's office and entered. After a bit they came out together and met Tredway almost in front of Hopalong's hideaway. Listening, he could hear every word of their conversation.

"Colonel," Lewis began, "Miss Blair has asked me to stop you from makin' any sale of those cows you got from the Picket Fork until this case is settled."

"That's ridiculous!" Tredway replied tartly. "They are my cattle. Anyway, you have no such authority."

"Reckon I do," Lewis drawled composedly. "I can impound 'em as evidence. You're not to sell the herd or any cow in it."

"What?" Tredway was furious. He needed money badly. "Don't be a preposterous fool! Of course I'll sell them!"

"Sorry, Colonel." Lewis's voice grew stern. "But you won't. If you do, I'll have to arrest you."

Tredway glared at Cindy, then he looked back at Lewis. "Just who are you supporting here? This passel of crooks or the townspeople?"

"I'm supportin' the law," Lewis replied easily, "like I was appointed to do. I aim to keep on supportin' it. You know, Tredway, there ain't but durned little evidence against these here folks. Mighty little. I'm holdin' 'em, but I'm huntin' more clues. It may be they ain't the right parties."

"There's no evidence that's worth paying attention to!" Cindy said. "I believe you stole my ranch, Colonel Tredway, and I think you were involved in the holdup of the stage."

"You accusing me?" He stared at her, his eyes malignant.

"Yes," she replied, "and when the case comes to court, we're going to have some evidence of our own to present. One of the best sources of evidence—an eyewitness to the thieves meeting someone just after the robbery. I think he will identify both you and Bill Saxx!"

Tredway's face flushed, then turned pale. Buck Lewis was staring at him, then looking at Cindy. "That's a serious charge, miss," he warned. "Can you prove it?"

"The witness," she said coolly, "was one of the Brothers from Babylon Mesa."

Tredway stiffened and he turned white as death. He stared at Cindy, only his eyes alive in the dead white of his face. "Woman, you are making wild accusations, and I've had about enough of it. Marshal Lewis would be very foolish to base any charges against me on the testimony of any one of that group of madmen."

Buck Lewis interrupted. "The order stands, Colonel. You sell none of those cattle until this thing is settled."

"But Cameron, Cassidy, whoever he is, failed to get the five hundred head before quitting. The cattle are mine according to the terms of the contract."

"We have the cattle," Cindy said calmly. "You owe Hopalong that money. He hid several hundred head in another corral—and you will live up to your contract!"

"To a lot of thieves?" Tredway demanded furiously.

"They might have got you there, Colonel," Lewis replied amiably. "The question of whether they are thieves ain't settled, but that don't make any difference, anyway. If they've got the cattle, they can collect—even if they are proved to be thieves."

Tredway relaxed slowly. If they did have more cattle and they could produce them, they could demand payment—and he did not have the money. But if they didn't have the cattle—

Suddenly he felt better. He smiled confidently. "Well, perhaps I overreacted. I'll admit I don't like the way these men have conducted themselves. If they have the cattle, naturally they will be paid. Sorry, Marshal, and you, too, Miss Blair, for my outburst."

They watched him walk away, and Lewis shook his head. "Now, what d'you think of that?" he demanded. "One minute he's mad enough to bite a cougar an' the next thing he's smooth as oil."

After they had departed, Hopalong sat very still in the abandoned building and considered what he had overheard. The answer was no puzzle to him, for the logical way to avoid payment was to send his riders out to move the cattle to some hideout that would not be known to Cassidy or his friends. Then, even if freed, they would fail to deliver and lose all claim to any money from Tredway.

By the way in which Tredway left, he was about to get things rolling to do just that, and Hopalong dared not leave. He could hear someone working behind the adjoining building, so escape that way was impossible. And the front opened on the street, where there were at least a dozen people within a hundred yards.

There was only one solution. He would wait and carry on as he had started. He would gain access to the hotel, and once inside, he would have a look for the hidden evidence. If he found it, then he would move against Tredway's men. There was nothing to do but sit and await darkness.

The hours dragged by, but finally dusk began to gather in the street. Anxiously he tried to calculate the time required to ride to the hidden corral in the pear forest. There was every chance they did not know where it was despite Tredway's previous knowledge of the vicinity, and they would lose time searching. Yet there were enough tracks if they could find them—but they could not see them at night! That was his best chance.

He dozed, and finally slept. He awakened with a start to find it completely dark. There were no lights in the hotel, none down the street except in one distant cabin and the lantern kept burning over the livery-stable door. Stiff from sleeping in his awkward position, Hopalong got to his feet and eased the bone-handled guns to an easier position on his hips. He moved to the door. A hinge creaked slightly, and then he was in the deep shadow of the doorway.

The street was empty. Down in front of the Elk Horn was a black spot that might be a sleeping dog. There was nothing else. For several minutes Hopalong studied the building fronts, their deepest shadows, their windows and doors. He detected no movement. It would do nothing but harm to be seen now and arrested. In jail he would be helpless. Thankful for his dark clothing, he moved from the shadows and crossed the street.

He did not run, knowing how a moving and especially a swiftly moving object draws the eye. When he was under the awning in front of the hotel, he paused again. The lobby was dark and empty. A light burned over the desk on which there was a bell to ring for the night clerk. He eased open the door and stepped in.

Swiftly Hopalong moved behind the desk and squatted on his haunches, studying the floor. The space was no more than six by six and framed by the counter behind him, the desk, safe, and pigeonholes for keys. On the floor there was nothing loose but the wastebasket. With a struck match he studied that floor with care, and found nothing.

The boards were even and smooth and dust filled all the cracks. Had he found one with less dust, he would have suspected it, but there was nothing here that offered a clue. He felt beneath the desk, under the safe, hoping the papers or whatever they were might be pasted to the bottom of one or the other, but he found nothing. He was about to give up when he saw something else. It was a break in the strip of molding that covered the crack where the floor and wall joined.

Kneeling, Hopalong inserted the point of his knife, and the piece lifted out easily. Below and behind it the crack had been widened with a sharp knife, and hanging to a nail was a string. Lifting it, Hopalong found at the end several long manila envelopes. Hastily he stuffed them inside his shirt and behind his belt. Then he straightened to his feet and stepped from behind the counter. As he did so he came face-to-face with Bill Saxx.

The big blond man stared from Hopalong to the counter, his eyes suspicious. "What're you doin' back there?"

"Checking the register," Hopalong replied quietly.

"Yeah?" Saxx had his hands on his hips, and he stared hard at Hopalong. "Wonder what the marshal will think of that? He's huntin' you for that holdup."

Cassidy never moved his eyes from Saxx. He was in for trouble and he could see no way to avoid it, although right now trouble was the very last thing he wanted.

"Whatever you got back there," Saxx said coolly, "I want it. Hand it over."

Hopalong smiled easily. "Now, that's foolish talk," he said, "for if I got anything, it is something I want and intend to keep."

Saxx swung from the hip, balling his fist as his hand shot out. The punch was hard and fast, thrown with all of his great strength. It was wrong only in one thing. It was a swing, and the straightest line is just that, a straight line, not a curved one. Hoppy's left leaped out in a stiff jab that caught Bill Saxx on the mouth and set him back on his heels. Instantly Hopalong stepped in and smashed a heavy right to the ribs and, rolling, hooked a hard left to the midsection. Hurt, Saxx staggered and hit the steps leading to the second floor. He came up with a lunge, swinging hard. Hopalong threw a right, missed, and the two men fell into a clinch. His left hand on Saxx's biceps, Hopalong caught the back of Saxx's right elbow and thrust his leg quickly behind the legs of the larger man and threw him to the floor. He hit with a thud that shook the building.

Furious, he lunged to his feet and hurled himself at Hopalong, who met him coming in with a smashing left. Saxx was a powerful man and he had been hurt, and suddenly all his innate viciousness came to the fore. Toe to toe they stood in the dim light of the lobby and slugged it out. Hopalong was lighter but faster, and he hit with the jarring force of a trip-hammer. Saxx took the punches coming in and smashed back, his heavy fists rocking Hopalong's head and jarring him clear to his heels. Slipping a wicked right, Hopalong smashed a left to the teeth, then whipped a right to the midsection and then slammed both hands to the head. Saxx ducked lower and bored in, but Hopalong uppercut hard and straightened him. Trying with a left for the face, Hopalong missed and fell into a right to the chin.

Lights seemed to explode, and the room spun. He felt himself falling, felt the smashing of blows to the head and body, and then he went down hard and rolled over. Hurt though he was, he knew he had to get to his feet, that on the floor he would be helpless before the boots of the big ranch foreman. Rolling over, Hopalong lunged to get up and moved just in time to miss the full force of Saxx's first kick. He went down again, however, and Saxx came after him. Helpless to rise fast enough, Hopalong rolled up to his shoulders, bracing his hips with both hands, and kicked out with both spurred heels. The first one raked Saxx across the face and the second ripped his shirt and drew blood on his arm. Saxx sprang back, cursing with pain, and Hopalong rolled over and came to his feet. Saxx charged, and Hopalong Cassidy met him with a left fist that loosened four front teeth. The foreman stopped in his tracks, and Hopalong whipped over a right that laid open the bigger man's face for three inches.

Shouts and inquiring yells rang out from all over the hotel and footsteps pounded on the hall floor upstairs. Hopalong was desperate. To be found here now meant arrest. He saw Bill Saxx boring in, his eyes ugly with pain and fury, and then Saxx swung hard with his left. Catching the blow on his forearm, Hopalong chopped wickedly at the Box T foreman's jaw. It was a short, vicious punch, and it hurt. Stopped in his tracks, half off balance, Saxx shook his head and started to lift his hands when Hopalong hit him, one-two on the chin. He went back, and Hopalong followed up with a looping, lifting bolo punch to the wind. With a grunt, Saxx folded and Hopalong uppercut hard with both hands. Footsteps sounded on the steps. Hopalong glanced once at the fallen man, then went through the door with a jump.

Disregarding the steps, he hit the street running, went between the buildings across the street, and gasping for breath, his lungs stabbing with pain, he raced for his horse. Behind him came yells and much loud talk. Slowly he eased his pace. His heart was pounding, his chest heaving. Somehow he had managed to grab up his hat, although he had no memory of it, and both guns were still in place. Glancing back, he saw no pursuit, and walked on, stones rolling under his boots occasionally. Sweat trickled into his eyes and they smarted with the salt.

His shirt was torn, his face bloody. His lip must have been split inside, for he could taste blood. He stopped once to mop the sweat from his face, and his breathing slowed down, his heart eased in its pounding. Evidently he had not been seen.

A few minutes later he had reached Topper and was in the saddle. He walked the horse back into the trees and, avoiding open places, moved over the ridge and to the lower ground beyond. It was a long ride to the camp on the Picket Fork, and he was suddenly very, very tired. He sagged in the saddle, his body moving with the easy rhythm of Topper's walking. His fingers strayed to his waistband. He still had the papers. If he swung wide of his trail, he could be at Burnside's before daybreak. It would increase the time taken to get to the camp, but no matter. These papers, whatever they were, should be in the hands of the old lawman. He turned Topper toward the ranch at Dead Horse Pass, then dozed in the saddle.

*　　*　　*

It was almost midafternoon before Hopalong neared the camp on the Picket Fork.

Almost at once he saw that the Box T hands had found the cattle. They were there, and with them several unknown Mexican riders. Vin Carter seemed to be in charge and they were moving the cattle out, gathering them on the south bank of the Picket Fork near the site of the old camp, ready to drive them on.

Alone, Hopalong rode from the timber. Vin Carter had gone back into the brush toward the drag end of the herd. Pres was the first to see him coming, and the cowhand cast one quick glance toward where Vin Carter had gone, then waited to meet Hopalong. Another Box T rider, Krug, had faced around also, and both men got down from their horses.

"Where you going with those cattle?" Hopalong demanded.

"Drivin' to the Box T," Pres said. "What did you expect?"

"You've no right to move them," Hopalong said. "They are our gather and will be moved when we're ready."

Pres shrugged insolently. "That's your worry. My orders are to move 'em. If you don't like that, talk to Vin. He'll straighten you out. In fact," the cowhand added, "I can't think of anything he might like better."

Hopalong dismounted, keeping Topper between them. Then he walked around the horse. A glance had told him the Mexican riders were holding aloof, watching with interest, but apparently with no idea of interference. "If you move them," Hopalong said, "I'll want a tally."

Pres shrugged again. "Then make your own tally. We got no such orders."

"All right." Hopalong was agreeable. "I'll do it." He hooked his thumbs in his belt. "If I were in your shoes, I'd be doing some serious thinking. Tredway's through. He can't protect you any longer."

"Yeah?" Pres stared at Hopalong. "Where did you get the idea that I needed any protection?"

"Just telling you." Hopalong shrugged. "Burnside didn't stop when he killed two of your boys. He's on the trail of the outlaws and he's got a good lead. You're trailing with the wrong crowd, Pres."

Unknown to Hopalong, Vin Carter had come from the chaparral behind him. Sighting Cassidy, the Box T segundo narrowed his eyes with calculation. Swinging from his horse, he took his rifle and worked his way around behind Hopalong. His eyes glued to the broad shoulders of the silver-haired rider, he was giving no thought to any danger to himself. Separated from the herd and standing half-hidden in the brush was a big black steer that had previously given Hopalong trouble. He was one of three who had fought hardest against capture, and now free, he stood in the mesquite, glaring red-eyed at the man slipping through the brush. His head came down and he pawed at the leaves.

Carter heard the sound and hesitated, listening. Behind him the black steer moved with all the silence of the stalking wild creature it had become. With Cassidy not fifty yards from him, Carter lifted his rifle and drew a careful bead on Hopalong's back. Nestling the rifle against his cheek, taking aim, Vin heard a faint rustle behind him. His head came around, and he glanced over his shoulder.

Whatever else he might be, Vin Carter was a cattleman, and no fool when it came to range stock. One glance at the big steer and he knew exactly how much danger he was facing. Yet in the crucial instant he froze, torn between the instinctive realization of his danger and his lust to kill Cassidy. And it was that hesitation which was to prove fatal.

The black steer weighed more than two thousand pounds and it was raw power, all mighty muscle and bone. The creature was scarcely ten yards from Vin Carter when the outlaw turned, and in that instant the big steer bunched his muscles and lunged, his great head of horns lowered.

With a cry, Vin swung his rifle and fired point-blank. Even had the bullet hit, nothing on earth could have stopped him, for the beast had every ounce of his strength gathered in this lunge at the hated man-thing that had driven him from his brushy stronghold, subjected him to the rope and the corral. Vin's rifle bellowed, and he tried to work the lever. One fleeting instant he jerked down on it and then the lowered head struck him.

He went flying back, his body striking a tree, then rebounding. The steer hooked low and hard, and Vin Carter screamed wildly as the horn tore into him.

The shot and the scream had followed one on the other. Wheeling, Hopalong saw the steer goring the man; he ran three quick steps to the left, his hand lifting iron. The steer lunged toward the fallen man again and Hopalong fired!

The big steer stumbled and went to his knees. Walking

swiftly forward, Hopalong fired again. That bullet struck the beast in the eye and he went over on his side, his legs kicking out in the throes of death.

Pres and Krug had rushed forward, followed by the Mexicans. Hopalong dropped beside the fallen man. He needed no telling as to what Vin Carter had planned here; the rifle was evidence enough.

Carter lay sprawled on the leaves, alive but dying. He looked up, no recognition in his eyes. "Never seen him!" he gasped. "He was right on me afore I . . . " His voice trailed away.

The Mexicans glanced at one another and crossed themselves. One picked up the rifle curiously and glanced at the situation, then inquiringly at Hopalong Cassidy. None of them spoke.

Hoppy got to his feet, his face grave. "Well, he asked for it," he said quietly.

Pres said nothing, and Krug only shifted his feet. Both men were obviously upset by the sudden death of the Box T segundo, and another thing that disturbed them was the flashing speed of Hopalong's draw. That draw could have been against them as well as this steer, and it would have meant death for one or both of them. It was a sobering thought. Both men were courageous enough, but it is one thing to face risk of death and quite another to face certainty of death. Pres was suddenly aware that there was nothing in Kachina that made him want to die.

"What happens now?" Krug asked suddenly, staring at Cassidy. "You said Tredway was through. Was that straight?"

"It is. Last night," Hopalong said quietly, "I got the only

evidence that was needed. I put it in the hands of the man who will use it. By now Tredway may be in jail."

"Where's Saxx?"

Hopalong shrugged. "How should I know? I saw him last night, and we had it out in the Mansion House lobby. I whipped him."

Pres scowled his disbelief. "You whipped Saxx?" He was incredulous. "That's never been done."

"It's been done now," Hopalong said dryly, "and for all I know, he may be in jail, too. What you do is up to you. But I'd turn those cattle into that big corral where we made our first gather, then I'd either give myself up or light out of the country. I've nothing," he added, "against you hombres. My quarrel's with Tredway."

Pres looked at Krug. The Mexicans had drawn away from them and were talking among themselves. Backing up, Hopalong swung into the saddle and turned the white horse toward Kachina.

Tom Burnside was nervously pacing the earthen floor of the livery stable and he strode to the doors as Hopalong swung down from Topper. "Man," he exclaimed excitedly, "am I glad to see you! There's strange doin's about."

"What do you mean?"

"Somebody claims they seen a ghost the last couple of nights. Sensible folks, too. They claim they seen a white-lookin' thing floatin' near the back of the Mansion House. When Tredway heard that, he was some upset. Some other folks claim they run into three of the Brothers dressed in those robes crossing the trail near Dead Horse Pass. Been some strangers in town, too. Two, three hombres, all with beards."

Hopalong nodded. "Now that makes some sense," he said. "It's the Brothers, from Babylon Mesa."

"Suppose they knowed him?" Burnside asked keenly. "If they did, what do they want with him?"

"No telling," Hopalong said. "About those papers. Did you look them over? Is there anything there?"

"Anything?" Burnside laughed. "I'll say there is! Some of the papers belonged to Pete Melford. Letters from the government about his land. Then there was other papers, an' among them a poster showin' John 'Fan' Harlan wanted for murder an' robbery. Evenas sure enough had the deadwood on Tredway. What beats me is why Tredway didn't get the papers from him before he killed Evenas."

"My idea is that he intended to, and Evenas made a break for it. On the way into town to get the papers, he made a break to get away and Tredway shot him."

"All right," Burnside said, "here comes Buck Lewis. Let's go face Tredway."

Lewis looked at Hopalong, then accepted the papers Burnside handed him. He nodded from time to time as he glanced over them. Finally he looked up. "This proves it as far as I'm concerned. I've dug up a few things m'self. That track you showed me, Tom, fit a pair of boots that belong to Tredway. The one down near the wagon. I figure you were right in guessin' that he planted that money on the Townes."

"If we look close," Hopalong said, "I think we'll find that he killed old man Peavey to keep him from talking. I think he was killed in the hotel, then dropped from the window sometime later."

Buck Lewis nodded. "That makes sense. Well, I don't mind sayin', boys, this here's the first time I ever arrested a man when it gave me pleasure. I'm an hombre that believes in live an' let live, but he's been a hard man about this town, hard on those as owed him. Let's go!"

They went, three tall Western men walking side by side, Hopalong Cassidy and the two pioneer lawmen. As they reached the door to the Mansion House, a bearded man across the street got to his feet. Then, casually, he drifted into the hotel entrance after them.

At Tredway's shout they opened the door and walked into his room. He looked quickly from one to the other, his lips thinning down, his face suddenly gaunt. "Well, what is it?"

"I'm arrestin' you, Tredway. Arrestin' you for murder, robbery, an' a few other charges."

Tredway leaned back in his chair. "What kind of nonsense is that?" he demanded. "You've no evidence."

Coolly Buck Lewis named off the papers he had, and slowly the older man's face turned gray and bitter. Perhaps not even he knew how Evenas had managed to get possession of these papers. Some of them obviously had been stolen from this office where the Colonel now sat. Others, like the affidavits, he must have ridden miles to get. Foolish as Evenas had been at the end, he had prepared his case well. There was evidence enough here to hang Tredway, or to send him up for life. From these papers a dozen charges could be built.

"Also," Lewis went on to say, "we tracked you to the Towne folks' wagon. We know you planted that unsigned an' stolen money on them. We also figure you killed old man Peavey. We may prove that an' may not. We can," he added, "prove that you killed Evenas.

"These here papers show he tried to blackmail you. Also, we found a smashed lamp in your house, an' spilled oil. That fits with the burns on the dead man. We've got you dead to rights."

Tredway sat silent for several minutes before replying. When he looked up, his eyes fastened on Cassidy. "It's you I have to thank for this," he said. "My trouble started when you came into this country. It was you I should have killed."

His eyes flickered to those of Lewis and Burnside. "I'm not through," he said, low-voiced. "I'm not through at all. I'll get out of this, or I'll get away. I can still beat you. And when I do," he said viciously, "I'll nail all your hides on the fence."

"You're just lucky," Hopalong said quietly, "that we got you first. There are others who want you."

Fear flickered in the hard eyes. Tredway's tongue touched his lips. He started to get to his feet, then sat back, looking nervously at Lewis. "All right," he said bitterly, "take me to your jail. I'll not stay there long!"

As Buck Lewis and Burnside started to leave with their prisoner, Hopalong called after them: "When you turn Pike and Rig loose, tell them to meet me across the street, will you?"

He walked over to the Chuck Wagon and sat down, accepting the cup of coffee that was put before him. Several men drifted in and sat down nearby. All were silent but friendly.

Suddenly the door opened and Pike stepped in with Tom Burnside behind him. "They got him, Hoppy!"

Cassidy came to his feet. "Who got who?"

"The Brothers. They got Tredway."

"What?"

All eyes were on Pike Towne. "Yeah, Lewis came in an' unlocked the door. He was puttin' him into the cell where I'd been when all of a sudden there's two men standin' in the door behind the marshal holdin' double-barrel shotguns. Then another gent comes in the back. All three are wearin' these home-spun robes with hoods.

"One of them is lookin' at the marshal, an' he says, 'We have a prior claim on this man. He is wanted by us for murder and robbery. I regret to say he was once one of our own and we handle our own affairs.'

"Buck looks at them and he looks at all that artillery. I reckon he decided there was no use takin' any chances. He wouldn't have had much of one, anyway."

Pike dropped on a bench. "There was a bunch more of them outside. They took him out of there, an' if you ever seen a man go to pieces, it was him.

"I tell you, he didn't do no more braggin'. His face was white as death an' he started to beg. Buck just looked at him, an' if I ever saw contempt on an hombre's face, it was on his. 'Go on, Tredway,' he says, 'you got to answer anyway. Maybe I should fight to keep you, but I don't want these hombres to have my blood on their souls over the likes of you. Nor of these other men.' He motions to Rig an' me. So they took him on out of there an' they rode off."

"What d'you think they'll do?" Rig asked.

Tom Burnside looked at him. "Man," he said, "I seen what them Penitentes do to themselves for religion. The good Lord only knows what they'll do to him. One thing I know—I wouldn't be in his boots for anything."

He turned suddenly to Cassidy. "Hoppy, one thing I've been wanting to tell you. You'd better watch your step. Bill Saxx blew town this mornin' an' he swears he'll have your hide."

CHAPTER 10

FAN HARLAN ESCAPES

Cindy Blair was waiting in the lobby with Sarah Towne beside her when Hopalong came in with Pike and Rig Taylor. Hoppy smiled at them and removed his hat. "Well, looks like you'll get your ranch. There was enough in those papers that Evenas had corralled to prove title for you."

"Thanks to you," she said quickly.

"Not me!" He shook his head. "You thank Rig here, and Pike. Although," he added, "I don't know that you've got much. That old PM is mighty fine grazing land, but you've no money."

"We'll have some," she replied quickly. "We can claim title to all the cattle you boys rounded up and sell them. Then we can pay you and still have money enough to start things going. We'll make out."

"There's only one thing worries me," Rig Taylor said. "I'm wondering what became of Bill Saxx and Tote Brown."

Hopalong had not forgotten them. All morning he had been remembering the big, tough foreman. Saxx would not take a beating so easily, and the money had not yet been found. It was sure to be on the ranch, and Buck Lewis had ridden out there. Of Tote Brown he knew nothing. It had probably been Tote who had fired on him the day of his visit to Babylon Mesa. He scowled, thinking about Buck Lewis. The marshal had ridden out there alone. "I think"—he got to his feet—"I'll take a ride out to the Box T myself."

As one person they turned to face him. "You think Lewis may run into Saxx?"

"I doubt it, but there's no telling what Saxx will do now. If he's smart, he'll ride right out of the country and keep on riding, just like Krug and Pres did."

"Are you sure they left?" Burnside asked skeptically. "If Saxx meets 'em, he'll talk 'em into stayin'. Mark my words."

"What do you suppose the Brothers wanted with Tredway?" Rig wondered.

"Once I've seen Lewis," Hopalong told them, "I'm going back up there. I've mentioned it to nobody except you who were concerned, but they had some reason for being interested in Tredway. I want to know what happens to him."

"I'll go along," Pike offered, getting to his feet.

"Nothing doing!" Cassidy refused help. "This is over for you, Pike. You've got Sarah to look after. This is my job from now on."

He went out along the boardwalk and swung into the saddle, starting Topper down the street toward the trail.

"I reckon," Pike said hesitantly, "nobody is better fitted to finish this off than he is, but just the same I'd like to ride along."

Hopalong put Topper to a rapid gait and rode for the Box

T. Dust puffed from Topper's hooves and there was no other sound but the creak of the saddle. Suddenly Hopalong saw buildings ahead, and in the ranch yard he could see a saddled horse standing, reins trailing. What made him worry he did not know, but he spoke to Topper, and the white gelding lunged into a fast run. He swept down the hill and Hopalong sprang from the horse and ran for the door, which stood open.

Buck Lewis lay sprawled on the floor, his leg bloody and a gun near his hand. Dropping to his knees, Hopalong turned the marshal over. Buck's eyes fluttered open and he stared up, trying to focus his attention. When he recognized Hopalong Cassidy, he tried to grin. "Reckon," he gasped, "I ketched one. It was that durn Bill Saxx. He was waitin' for me when I come down the hill. He didn't get the money, but he beat me to the gun an' lit out for the hills."

"You aren't hit bad." Hopalong had been swiftly checking the wounds. "You took one through the leg. I think you'll be all right, but you'd better start back for town."

"I reckon I can make it. You goin' after him?" Buck Lewis hesitated, then he said, "Maybe you'd better, Hoppy. Sure, I never wanted any man shot, but Saxx has gone plumb wild. He swore to me that he'd kill all of you, but it was Rig an' yourself he wanted most."

Cindy and Rig with their newfound happiness, and Pike and Sarah able to find some peace at last. It would never do for Bill Saxx to be at large.

Hopalong checked his guns, then turned toward his horse. "See you, Buck!" He waved a hand, then walked his horse from the yard.

Too experienced with bad men to be fooled, Hopalong Cassidy knew just what he was facing. Bill Saxx was a known gunman, dangerous under any conditions but now furious over his beating and the defeat of all their plans. If he came in contact with Krug and Pres, they would have no choice but to join him or fight it out. He would accept no arguments. So while he was trailing one man he must also be prepared to meet three.

Sure in his knowledge of the ways of hunted men, Hopalong believed that Saxx would head for the pear forest and either hide out there or lose his trail in its depths. Then, if he wished to get away, he might ride down the old trail past Brushy Knoll and into the almost trackless wilderness beyond. Certain it was that the trail Hopalong now found was heading straight for the Picket Fork. Beyond the stream he would have water and beef for the killing. Living would be easy enough, and Saxx would be able to strike from there at his enemies. Without doubt there were people in Kachina who would help him out of fear or the hope of profit.

Knowing the man, Hopalong Cassidy knew what a ruthless and relentless enemy he would be. Fiercely proud, he had taken an unmerciful beating in public. Over and above the fact that the holdup had proved profitless to him and the money lost. He had shot and, he would believe, killed the marshal. From foreman of the biggest ranch in the area, he had become a fugitive and an outlaw. No man, not even Tredway himself, could be more dangerous.

The corral where the cattle had been gathered looked lonely now, and the fire where their meals had been cooked was only long-dead ashes and blackened stones. There is nothing so forlorn as a deserted and long-dead campfire where one has been with friends. The trail left by Bill Saxx did not pause near the camp, but continued on across the Picket Fork. His guns loose in their holsters, Hopalong rode into the pear forest, every sense alert to danger.

Shadows were deep, and he rode slowly, his ears attuned to the slightest sound. He knew that he might hunt for days without finding the former Box T foreman. And the man was skilled in woods travel and in mountains or plains.

As if sensing the alertness of his master, Topper stepped daintily as he crossed the stream and entered the pear forest, ears up and twitching. It was very still. The sun's heat was thickened by the unmoving air and seemed to settle down and gather in the small open places. He rode slowly and with many pauses to listen. In the dust beneath the chaparral Topper's hooves made little sound, but listen as he might, Hopalong could hear nothing. Yet here and there he found a track, and he knew that somewhere ahead of him was Saxx.

Did the outlaw know he was followed? Hopalong doubted it, yet there was a chance, and if he knew he was followed by one man alone, he would not wait long for a meeting.

Cindy Blair was starting up the path from the bottoms when she saw the horse. Rig had gone off somewhere to hunt up Buck Lewis and see how he was getting along, and she had suddenly remembered there was no coffee in the Towne wagon. With a word to Sarah she had saddled her mare and started out of the bottoms to pick up supplies, the same supplies they had been forced to leave behind when Sarah's only money had proven to be stolen.

The horse was standing in the trail, and he seemed to have a pack on his back. Also, there was something wet and glistening on his shoulder. Puzzled and worried, she turned her horse back along the lip of the wash toward the trail. When next she sighted the horse, she felt a start of fear. On the horse's back was a man!

He was bent far forward, and the horse's shoulder was bloody and red. The man looked strange. Even as she rode up to him he slid from the saddle and fell heavily into the road. Swinging down, Cindy ran to the man, and then saw what made him look so different. He was dressed in a homespun cloak and hood. His chest and stomach were literally drenched in blood and his shirt soaked with it. Gently she stretched the man out on the grass beside the road, then she lifted his head and removed the hood.

He was a fair-haired young man, and now his face was very pale. Yet she saw at once that he was conscious. His eyes flickered open. "Harlan . . . got . . . " he whispered hoarsely. His lips fluttered and worked hard at the words. "Got . . . got away!"

Suddenly Cindy was frightened. Desperately she worked over the man, finding his wounds, of which there were four, and bathing them as well as she could with water from her canteen, then she ripped up her skirt and bandaged the wounds. Obviously the man had started back to town for help and had fainted when almost there. He had lost his grip on the bridle reins, they had fallen to the ground, and the horse had stopped, as trained.

When the man was resting more comfortably, she stepped

quickly to the side of the road. Drawing her rifle from the scabbard, she fired three fast shots, waited an instant, then fired three more. Hastily she reloaded, and was rewarded by a rush of horses' hooves, racing from the town.

Rig Taylor was the first to arrive, and behind him were Pike Towne, Tom Burnside, and several others. Quickly she told her story. When she had finished, the man on the ground gasped out the details.

They had been nearing Babylon Mesa. Several men had ridden on ahead with the prisoner. He and one other had been bringing up the rear. Suddenly there was a commotion ahead and they had rushed forward to run into a blast of gunfire. His companion had been killed instantly, but his own horse had bolted with him clinging to the saddle.

Knowing he could never get up the trail in his present condition, he had turned his horse and started back for town. All five of the men guarding Tredway had been killed. Whether the advance group had turned back he did not know. His one thought had been to prevent the escape of the killers.

"How many was there?" Pike demanded.

"Don't know. Maybe—maybe three, four."

Pike's face was serious. "Three or four. That means Bill Saxx may have caught up with Krug an' Pres. Now Tredway is with 'em. They are on the dodge, an' they'll be feelin' mighty mean."

"We'd better get going," Rig said gravely. "We'll get this man back to town to the doc, then we'll get a posse and head out down the trail."

Cindy Blair watched them go, walking to her own horse.

They had rushed off to send a buckboard for the wounded man, and it was not until she had led the mare back to the shade near him that she thought of Hopalong.

He was out there alone, hunting Bill Saxx. He would find himself facing four or five men, Tredway among them, and he would have no warning! Frightened, she sprang into the saddle. The wounded man looked up at her. "You'll be all right," she said quickly. "They are coming for you. Hopalong Cassidy is hunting for one man—he'll find four. They'll kill him!"

The little mare was a runner and liked it. She took to the trail like a rabbit. Cindy's mind flashed ahead. Hopalong had gotten into this because of her, to help her. They had not found the PM steers he wanted, but he had found evidence to prove her claim, and now he was riding unwarned into a trap. He would never dream that Tredway was free.

He would go to their old camp, she was sure of that. Her own knowledge of the West was good, and she had hunted too much not to know that a hunted man will head for shelter. Saxx would avoid open country, try to lose his trail. He would go for the chaparral and Hopalong would follow him. But Saxx had already struck from the chaparral to free Tredway, who had been longer in the country than any of them and who would know more of the thickets than anyone else.

After a fast start she slowed the game little mare to a space-eating trot and cut across country, taking every possible shortcut to cover the distance as quickly as possible. As she rode she tried to guess how far Hopalong would have penetrated into the pear forest and where he would be now.

She waded her horse across the Picket Fork and drove into

the brush. There was no trail at this point, but she hit it flat as she had seen Hopalong do and was soon pushing her way through. Branches tore at her, ripping her blouse and snagging her hair. She forced her way into a narrow cattle trail and turned along it, riding full tilt. Suddenly the trail opened, almost without warning, into a clearing. She was riding too fast to stop quickly, and before she realized what had happened, her mare had plunged into a group of horsemen. A hand shot out and grasped her bridle and she found herself looking into the eyes of Bill Saxx. He was grinning widely.

"Well, what d' you know?" He grinned, winking at Tredway. "We got company! Where you goin' in the hurry, ma'am?"

Cindy felt despair rise within her, then fear. These men were already outlaws. They were already murderers, and she could expect no mercy. One more crime, or a dozen more crimes, would mean nothing at all now. "Let me go," she said quietly. "Let go of that bridle!"

Saxx chuckled. "Let go? Honey, I always did figure on seein' a sight more of you."

Tredway turned impatiently. "Bring her along then, but let's move!"

"Bring her along?" Saxx chuckled again. "I'll say! She'll be good company, and she'll be bait for Cassidy, too."

Tredway nodded. "Let's get moving. Once we're where I'm taking you, we'll be safe enough. We can make Cassidy come to us as we like. And when we like."

Cindy's rifle was jerked from its scabbard and Pres tied a thong to her wrists and passed the other end to Saxx. Then they started on.

*　　*　　*

Dusk had fallen before Hopalong finally halted. He had lost the trail more than an hour before as several of the roving half-wild cattle had obliterated all evidence of the passing of the horseman. Yet he had continued on, following the paths that led deeper into the brush and hoping he was still on the trail.

Earlier in the day he had believed he heard distant shots, but in that clear and soundless air, they might well have carried for several miles and might have been fired at a coyote. They were not repeated, and he was not sure whether he had even heard the shooting or not. Having no desire to stop in the narrow paths of the pear forest, he continued even after the stars came out. Topper was a weary horse and Hopalong himself was sagging in the saddle, not so much from the riding of the day as from the accumulated fatigue.

Despite that, he grew more and more wary as the hours drew on, and when he approached a clearing, he hesitated and listened for a long time. He passed several of the cattle and finally bedded down near a seep of water on the far side. He was awake at the first gray of day and swiftly saddled Topper. The white gelding had rested and seemed in fine fettle. Mounting up, Hopalong started out once more.

He had gone no more than a mile when suddenly he drew up sharply. The track of Bill Saxx's horse was plain and clear, but accompanying it, the tracks evidently made the night before, were the hoofprints of four other horses! Dropping to the ground, Hopalong shoved his hat back on his head and studied the tracks.

As he did so his face grew serious. Getting to his feet, he walked on along the trail, leading Topper. Several times he paused to examine tracks, then when he stopped at last, his face was hard with worry and anger.

Pres was once more with Saxx. The track of the paint he rode most often was easily identified. That helped with some of the strange tracks also, for one of the other riders would be Krug. He had recognized the track of Cindy's mare at once, and the other track was the one made by the horse Tredway had ridden out of Kachina!

Tredway was free.

Tredway was free, and the outlaws had Cindy Blair a prisoner. That they would try to kidnap her seemed doubtful, but since she was with them, and from a boot track seen at one point during a brief halt Hopalong knew it was actually she, it was obvious that she had run into them by accident or some such thing.

There were no signs of any pursuers. So what could have happened? Apparently, he guessed, Saxx and his two companions had effected a delivery for Tredway.

As Topper walked on, Hopalong realized that his problem now was enormous. Saxx or Tredway were a match for any man, and together, aided by the other two, they made any attack or fight with less than their number dangerous and foolhardy. Yet he dared not turn back. The girl could not be left in their hands, and he would have to follow and trust to improvising some solution.

It was late afternoon before Hopalong Cassidy lost the trail. It had been following the canyon of Chimney Creek for more than a mile when suddenly he realized there were no more tracks in the dust. He dismounted and backtracked, working carefully. Until now the party had moved without hesitation, bound for some definite goal.

Now . . . ?

Twice he had worked along the trail before he found the white scar made by a shod horse on the face of a flat rock. Puzzled, he glanced in that direction and could see nothing but a short space of almost smooth rock to the very lip of the canyon. Walking out upon it, he glanced down and caught his breath. A steep trail dipped down on the very rim of the canyon, but a hoof mark showed itself plainly in a spot where dust had packed into a space between rocks. He was about to advance when wind whipped past his face and he heard the not-too-distant report of a rifle!

Diving for the brush, he heard a second shot and hit the trees running, then skidded to a halt. The shots had come from his own side of the canyon, and from the rim. Leaving Topper, he slipped his rifle from the boot and started out, skirting the rim of the canyon, then swinging wide to encircle the unknown antagonist. Almost instantly a shot clipped leaves near his head and he hit the dirt on hands and knees.

His tactics had been surmised and the man was ready for him. Hoppy lay still, studying the situation. Unless the marksman had moved, he was not more than fifty yards away and in a cluster of rocks that formed a rugged natural tower on the canyon rim. And that place presented problems for an attacker.

Yet Hopalong moved forward at once, weaving back and forth in the brush. Once he picked up a rock and tossed it to one side, but it drew no answering fire.

He studied an open space that ran between the clumps of brush, an open space that had grass all of a foot high in it. The grass might have been a trifle higher, he decided. He looked down at his own clothes. They were now covered with dust and streaked with sweat. They would, he decided, fade into the grass and rocks very easily. Moreover, the open alley between the lines of brush could not be overlooked by the watcher. He could see along it but could not look down upon it. Hoppy decided to take the risk of advancing along that open space. The chances were that his enemy would be searching the brush for movement and would not guess that Hopalong was approaching by the one place that seemingly offered no concealment at all.

Dropping to his stomach, Hopalong wormed his way out of the brush and headed toward the chimney of rocks. For an instant he lay still in a cold sweat. If he was seen here, he was cold turkey, and the worst of it was the man might wait until he was fairly close, deliberately letting him advance to his death.

Hopalong started forward, inching his way along the ground but keeping his head low. The man might be shrewd enough to watch that particular place, for any soldier or Indian fighter would know that it takes only a few inches of cover to hide a man if he lies still. And Hoppy was gambling that his movements would be slow enough to offer almost the same effect.

No sound came from the rocks. Hopalong's cheek was pressed to the earth to keep his head lower, and he tried to keep his body in a logical place for a rock to lie if the watcher happened to look that way. Whoever the man was he had been left behind to prevent Hopalong's following the party, and Cassidy was confident that the hideout was someplace near, possibly even in the ⸽om of the canyon itself.

He inched on, waiting for a long time at each stopping point. Having the patience of an Indian, he knew that haste is more often death than otherwise under these circumstances. Once, where the grass grew taller, he turned his head and peered forward. He was right out in the open now, none of the taller brush was anywhere close to him, and the rocks were not many yards away.

He lowered his head and crept on, making for an outcropping of chaparral that stood between him and the rocks. When he made it, he found the brush concealed a pile of rocks, and he rested there, studying the tower before him. On his side it was sheer, rising at least twenty feet above the terrain, but even though it could not be scaled from this side, neither could it offer any good spot for observation. He had managed to work his way halfway around the tower so that he was well on the other side from where he had last drawn fire.

Worming his way on, he finally took a chance, braced his toes in the sod, and came up with a rush that carried him into the shadow of the tower. If he had been seen, there was no evidence of it from the watcher.

Yet that man knew Hopalong was down here somewhere, and as long as he was out of sight, the watcher would grow increasingly nervous. Hopalong worked his way through the rocks around the tower toward the rim of the canyon. Hearing a slight noise, he froze in position, his Winchester at his hip. For an instant he stood still, then heard a second noise and at once he relaxed. Easing around a rock, he saw a small hollow, scarcely larger than a box stall, and there, cropping grass, was the bandit's horse, a fine-looking gray, dappled over the shoulders and hips.

Crossing the hollow with a low word to the horse, who merely looked curious and went back to cropping grass, Hopalong found himself looking up a notch in the rock. Yet almost as he glanced up the watcher above dropped into the crack and started scrambling down. Evidently he had no desire to wait and be trapped.

Drawing back, Hopalong waited. The man was Krug, and he came out of the crack almost at a trot. He was starting for his horse when Hopalong spoke. "Let go your gun belt, Krug."

The man's shoulders hunched as from a blow, and slowly he turned. Bitterly he glared at Hopalong. "I was a durned fool! Should have kept goin' when I had the chance!"

"That's right," Cassidy agreed. "Now drop your guns."

Reluctantly, but with careful hands, Krug unbuckled his belt and stepped back. "Believe it if you want to," he said, "but I was fixin' to slope. I'd been settin' up there watchin' for you, an' thinkin'. Then I saw you were out there, an' until I lost you, I figured to make a fight of it. All I wanted when I started for my horse was to get up an' get out."

"Sorry." Hopalong was stern. "You had your chance."

Turning the man around, Hopalong tied his hands, then

tripped him up and bound his feet, rolling him into the shade of a boulder. "What if you don't come back?" he pleaded. "Suppose they get you?"

Hopalong did not relent. "Then I'd say you were in a bad spot."

He squatted on his haunches. "Where are they? You're going to be tried for that stage holdup, but if you tell me, I'll put in a good word. I can't do more than that now."

"Reckon you can't." Krug was silent. "They got that Blair girl. She rode right into us. I don't hold with that. She's a fine person, but I knew better than tryin' to reason with Saxx or Tredway." He was silent again. "I never been to the place. All I know is that a canyon branches off Chimney Creek a ways up. No water in it most of the time, but a mile or so up, there's a good spring an' a water hole. There's shelvin' cliffs all along there an' plenty of shelter. I think they mean to hole up there while decidin' what to do next."

An hour later Hopalong and Topper had reached the bottom of Chimney Creek Canyon and were slowly moving up the canyon. At this point it was no more than two hundred feet deep and could be climbed at almost any point by a man on foot. He glimpsed no trails that would allow a horse to travel. The tracks of the outlaws were only occasionally to be glimpsed, but there was now no way for them to escape from the canyon.

He eased up and let Topper drink from a small pool of water that had gathered in the shade of the slope. From here on he must proceed with the utmost caution, for the men he pursued could be waiting around any rock or turn in the narrow canyon. He shoved his hat back and wiped his forehead with his bandanna. As he looked at the slope above the pool he saw something strange.

A boot.

It was hanging over the edge of a large rock just thirty feet away and the way that the heel stuck out indicated that there was a foot in it!

Moving slowly so as not to betray his alarm, Hopalong dismounted and slipped the thongs off of his six-guns. His mind racing, he walked to the shallow place where the water had collected. There was no cover! The rock with the man on top of it was near, very near. No doubt if the ambusher had moved to peer over the rock edge, Hopalong would have seen him immediately; it was only his protruding foot that had offered a warning. If he continued on either up or down the canyon, it was certain that he would end up shot in the back; it was only the hidden man's unwillingness to take on a man who was approaching his position that had saved him so far.

Unable to think of a better plan, Hopalong took a deep breath and shucked one of his guns. "All right, Topper," he said clearly and loudly, "let's move on."

Then he whirled, and hit the slope running as fast as he could! Rocks and dirt slid as he scrambled up, his gun held in front of him in one hand, the other grasping at brush and boulders for handholds as he climbed. As he came up over the edge of the rock where the unseen man was bedded down, he knew that fast as he was he had climbed too slowly and made far too much noise. He thumbed back the hammer of his gun and braced himself to take a bullet.

The man lay sprawled on the rock ledge, facedown. He had

not moved. Hoppy straightened and stood over him, sucking deep breaths and trying to steady himself. The man he had thought was a hidden ambusher was already dead!

Torn brush and furrowed earth on the slope above showed that he had fallen while making his way down into the canyon. The angle of his neck to his shoulders was so extreme that it must have been broken when he hit the rock ledge. Hopalong holstered the gun and turned the man over. It was the man he had seen in Kachina, the man Pike had told him was Tote Brown. Dried blood on his jaw indicated that he had been dead for many hours, if not days.

Hopalong Cassidy sat on the edge of the rock looking down at Topper. He waited until his pulse had returned to normal before sliding back down to the pool, mounting his horse, and continuing his cautious way up the canyon.

He heard them before he saw them. It was a sound of voices and the sharp crack of a breaking stick. Looking hurriedly about him, he saw a gap in a mass of mountain mahogany that covered one area near the north wall of the canyon. Leading Topper back into the gap, he found a space some dozen feet across with a little grass and plenty of cover. Tying Topper, Hopalong switched his boots for a pair of moccasins he always carried, and taking his rifle and canteen, he slipped out and started up the canyon wall.

When he could overlook their camp, he saw at once that they had an almost impregnable position. The country above the canyon walls was wild and lonely, a region of jumbled boulders, scattered juniper, and that look an untrammeled country has. He was now, he could see, west of Brushy Knoll. Babylon Mesa was behind him and ran off to the north, a towering wall of rock; this country was wild, uninhabited, and virtually unknown.

The canyon deepened and narrowed, and the walls grew steeper. If there was any way into that canyon but the way he had come, it was not visible, nor was there any indication of an entrance. Almost below him was the camp. He could smell the smoke, he could dimly hear the voices, but he could see nothing from where he lay. Below him there was the sound of running water and a freshness that comes only from the presence of water and vegetation.

As he lay there he began to plan, searching every corner of his mind for an idea. To face the lot of them would be useless and would only mean failure and death. Neither Tredway nor Saxx would hesitate to take a chance, and while he might get one of them, he would not get the other. And there were still three men down there, dangerous, hunted men, at least two of them killers.

He moved closer to the rim, listening. Voices came to him faintly at first, then clearer.

Cindy Blair was thoroughly frightened. She was courageous, used to the harshness of Western life; she understood her own situation better than most women could have. She knew the manner of men who held her prisoner, and knew none of them was to be trusted. If there was any hope, it lay in Pres, but he was the least forceful of the lot and the least likely to help her even if he wished. Krug had remained to kill Hopalong Cassidy. The fact that several shots had been heard disturbed the outlaws.

"Aw, he'll get him!" Saxx protested to Tredway. "He was probably just finishing Cassidy off."

Tredway's face seemed to have thinned down and grown more hawklike. His eyes were bitter and lighted by something else, something wild and dangerous. "Then where is he? One shot's all you need!" he snapped angrily. "I should have stayed there myself!"

Pres looked from one to the other. "What'll them Brothers do?" he asked cautiously.

Tredway advanced on him, his eyes vicious. "Do? What do you think they'll do? They'll come out of their holes like a pack of wolves, that's what! And make up your minds to this! If they get us now, it will be all of us, not just me!"

"What did they want you for?" Saxx asked.

"None of your business!" Tredway wheeled on him, half-crouched. "When I want questions from you, I'll ask for them!"

Bill Saxx gave Tredway a cold, measuring glance. "That's no way to talk," he said calmly. "We're all in this together. I don't aim to take that kind of talk. I don't work for you any longer, an' I didn't spring you from the Brothers to start taking orders again."

The eyes of the two men held. That weird look in Tredway's eyes disturbed Saxx, but he did not show it. The men glared at each other, and then Pres spoke up. "Aw, forget it! Why start fightin' among ourselves? We got troubles enough!"

Tredway relaxed slowly, then shrugged. "That's right. Sorry, Bill."

Saxx watched him as he turned away, and he was puzzled. He had never seen Tredway flash a gun on anybody, although he had seen him shoot, and he was good. Very good. But right then he would have sworn the boss was a gunman. That quick turn, the poised right hand, the left . . . He scowled. That left hand had been across in front of Tredway, poised palm down.

It came to him suddenly. He had seen such a pose once before. The man using it had been a gun fanner.

Cindy Blair had seen it, too, and she also had recognized it for what it was. From Rig and Pike she had heard the stories of the Ben Hardy gang, and suddenly she was looking at Tredway with new, attentive eyes. She added more fuel to the fire, and when the coffee started to bubble, she dished up the rest of the food they had forced her to prepare.

Tredway had walked some fifty feet away and was staring down the canyon. Under her breath Cindy said to Bill Saxx, "Be careful, he's killed a dozen men."

Saxx turned sharply and stared at her. "How do you know? You know more about my own boss than I do."

"I think I do. Hopalong Cassidy told me. Tredway used to run with the Hardy gang."

Bill Saxx's eyes narrowed to slits as he considered that.

Tredway came striding back to the fire. "Might as well eat," he said. "No sign of Krug. He must be all right. Cassidy couldn't get at him if he stayed in those rocks."

The hours dragged by and Tredway grew increasingly restless. Bill Saxx watched him with care, even while eating. Pres looked haunted and his eyes kept searching the rim of the canyon. He swore under his breath, smoked endless cigarettes, and paced nervously.

Saxx finally lay down and slept a little, and when he awakened it was night and the stars were out. Pres sat sullenly over the fire, but Tredway was gone.

Saxx sat up quickly. "Where is he?"

Pres nodded downcanyon. "Went to have a look. He's some worked up. He ain't near so worried about Cassidy as he is about the Brothers. He says they've got trackers among them who could follow an Apache upstream through a dust storm."

Saxx glanced at Cindy. She looked tired, although she had combed out her hair and made some effort to tidy up. "What did you tip me off about him for?"

She turned toward him. "Because you can be reasoned with. He can't be talked to now. He's crazy."

"Crazy?"

"Haven't you noticed his eyes? I think it was something about the Brothers Penitentes. They wanted him very badly for something that happened long ago, and he's afraid of them—deathly afraid. And right now he's in a killing mood."

"I'm not afraid of him. If he wants trouble, let him start it. I'm fed up with him pushing me around." Saxx was surly. "Thanks, though. You tipped me off. I won't forget that."

"He'll kill me." Cindy knew she was telling the truth. "He's mean. He's trapped now and he knows it, so he'll strike out at anything near him."

"Trapped?" Saxx was impatient. "What kind of talk is that? We're not trapped."

"Aren't you? You can't go downcanyon. They will be looking for you. By now the Brothers will be out in force, and Buck Lewis will have a posse. You can go on up the canyon, but you only have food for a few days. One man or two men might make it. Four never could. If you want to get away, you have to turn me loose."

Saxx grinned at her. "Smart, ain't you?" His eyes were speculative. "Get rid of another man, too? Ain't that what you said? Who'll it be?" He glanced at the sullen Pres. "This cowhand or Tredway?"

"It will be you or Tredway," Cindy replied quietly, "and you know it. You can get along with Pres. He's loyal and easygoing. He's used to working with you. Neither of you could get along with Tredway."

Saxx started to speak, and then the words froze on his lips. Justin Tredway stood across the fire, just on the edge of darkness. His eyes were on Bill Saxx, but he took in the whole camp as he spoke. "Get rid of me? Is that the idea? I'm crazy, am I?" He smiled, his lips breaking back over his teeth. "I'll give you cause to regret that, Miss Blair!" The voice was low and ugly, and the "Miss" was faintly emphasized with a sneer.

Saxx had not taken his eyes from Tredway, but now his former boss turned away with a shrug. He turned, and then there was a blast of fire from in front of him and Bill Saxx turned halfway around and felt blood covering his side.

Tredway looked at him, still holding the smoking derringer. "I was as fast as he was," he said quietly, "I think. But why gamble?"

Pres had remained sitting on the rock, too astonished to move. He looked down at the gun in Tredway's hand and remained riveted to his place, knowing a movement would mean certain death. Tredway turned his eyes then and looked at Cindy. Thinking to distract him, she spoke quickly. "You did take my ranch. The PM."

The remark made him frown, then he laughed shortly. "Of course. That old fool was in my way. I knew somebody would come looking for it, so I moved all the buildings down to the Box T, piece by piece, with my freight wagons. I had several drivers and outfits here from Virginia City right then and they did the work. Then I had a big cottonwood dug up and transplanted to the exact site of the house, and all the postholes filled, every sign of habitation removed, and even sod moved to cover some of the worn spots. The hardest thing was getting water to that tree and cutting back the branches."

"That was clever," Cindy said quietly. "Did you kill my uncle?"

"He was in the way."

He turned toward Pres and hesitated, staring at him through a long minute while Pres sat very still, his hands on his knees. "Get the horses," Tredway said, then: "We're moving out."

Pres got slowly to his feet and started toward the horses. A moment later they heard him saddling up. Tredway relaxed slowly and glanced once toward the body of Bill Saxx, lying in the shadows beyond the edge of firelight. "You'll come with me," he said to Cindy. "I'll need you. And don't get any hopes because Cassidy is around. He won't be able to help you. He's someplace on the rim—I trailed him that far. He won't be able to follow us because I've freed his horse and driven him off."

"You think that will stop him?" Cindy's eyes were contemptuous as she gazed at Tredway. "You always did underrate other men. That's been your trouble. You always believed you were a little smarter or a little faster, but when the chips were down, you always took the cheap way out."

He swung on her, his eyes blazing. "Shut up!" he said furiously.

"Like when you shot Bill Saxx. You were afraid to face him even up. *Afraid!*"

With a bound he was beside her, his hand drawn back to strike. At that instant there was a sudden clatter of horse's hooves, then a shout, "So long, Tredway!" The cry echoed against the rock walls, then died out.

Tredway forgot Cindy. He rushed to the edge of the firelight, hesitated, then plunged into the darkness. He was back before the girl could run. "He's gone!" he raged. "He ran off and left me! The yellow dog!"

"Not yellow," Cindy said coolly, "just smart. He knows you're through. Cassidy will get you, and if he doesn't, the Brothers will."

Their name brought him up short, and grabbing the girl by the wrist, he dragged her toward the horses. With her standing by him, he saddled quickly. Cindy's eyes kept going to the fallen Saxx. His guns had not been removed. If she could get one of them . . .

But he was watching her now, and he seemed to have detected some glance of hers. When the horses were saddled, he ordered her to mount. "There's a way out," he said grimly. "Let's go!"

"You'd better let me go," she told him calmly, concealing her fear. "I'll just be in your way."

"No," he said, and mounted his horse, turning up the canyon and away from the camp. Only once did he glance back, and then it was to see nothing but the flickering fire. All around was darkness.

Hopalong Cassidy was having his own troubles. He had been able to find no way to get down into the canyon from higher up and returned to overlook the camp once more.

Returning to the prisoner, he gave Krug a drink, then went back down the canyon. While still short of the bottom, he heard the shot. Hurrying, he climbed the wall again, but this time did not advance so far. A glance at the camp told him the story. Bill Saxx was down. He had been shot by Tredway. He was on the rim during Tredway's talk with Cindy, but while he could see them easily, he could not hear what they were saying. Earlier, he had missed Tredway by seconds only, for even as he had left his horse Tredway came up to him. As Hopalong had climbed the canyon wall the outlaw was turning Topper loose. Hopalong did not hear the clatter of hooves as Topper ran off, pursued by stones thrown by Tredway.

Now, as they mounted, he got hastily to his feet, debating whether to risk a shot, but Tredway was moving quickly and Cindy's position put her too close to the line of fire.

Scrambling down the cliff, Hopalong raced to where he had

left Topper. He hesitated to whistle, then tried it, but there was no sound and no response.

Circling, for the canyon swung wide at the point where Topper had been left, Hopalong followed the canyon to the campsite. When almost up to the fire, he stopped suddenly. Something was wrong! He glanced swiftly around, trying to see what. Bill Saxx was gone!

"Lookin' for me, Cassidy?"

Hoppy looked up to see Saxx standing under the shelving rock. His side bloody and his jaw was badly scraped, the foreman shifted unsteadily on his feet. "He suckered me with a hideout gun," Saxx said contemptuously. "I'm gonna kill you, Hopalong, an' then I'll hunt down that yellow belly an' take care of him." He stared somberly at Cassidy. "If it'll make you feel any better, I'll be turnin' that girl loose. She tipped me off on Tredway. Told me who he was."

"So you know then?"

"I know. That don't change what's between us, Cassidy. You whipped me—I don't take that from any man."

He stepped forward again, his eyes cold. "They say you're fast. Well, let's see!" His hand dropped with incredible speed and his gun came up roaring, but his first shot went far wild.

Hopalong Cassidy had drawn his gun as he always drew, with flashing, incredible speed. Once his hand was empty, then filled, and the gun blasting death. His first shot was a split second before Saxx fired. It struck, smashing through bone and tissue, turning Saxx halfway around with its force and sending the outlaw's bullet off into the night. Saxx swung back, his eyes blazing with cold fury. He fired, and Hopalong felt death brush his face, and then Hopalong fired again and again. The bullets smashed Saxx back on his heels. The last one broke his right arm. Switching the gun to his left hand, Saxx fired. He was falling as he pulled the trigger, and he followed his own last bullet to the ground. The gun fired once as he lay upon it, a muffled sound.

Cassidy fed cartridges into his gun and holstered it. Another tough man who had gone down a wrong trail. Why couldn't they see?

He turned away and started down the canyon calling for Topper. After some time he stopped and listened but heard nothing. He had almost given up and was considering climbing out of the canyon and going after Krug's mount, which had been left back at the ambush position at the head of the canyon trail, when he heard a movement in the brush. He called out again and then he heard a hoof click on stone and Topper appeared down the canyon, a white smear in the darkness.

"Come on, boy!" The horse trotted up, ears pricked. "There you are, you're a good old horse." Hopalong stroked his mane and then swung into the saddle.

There was a trail he found that left the canyon and he followed it up, and when dawn came at last, he circled wide and located the trail of two horses, striking off into wilder and wilder country.

The rocks grew more barren, and as the sun rose the land turned to fire. The grass fell behind and there were no more trees. On and on they pressed with the sun boiling down, and

Hopalong's lips cracked and his eyes worked at the distant heat haze, trying to find a sight of the two he followed.

His shirt grew darker with sweat, the stubble of beard on his cheeks gathered dust, and his eyes were ever busy, never flagging in their quest. The heat was a living thing, and he touched his lips only a little with the water in his canteen, then pushed on. Dust devils danced across a vast, empty distance marked by nothing but the trail of two riders. And then out of the north came another trail, a trail of several riders that moved in and obliterated the trail they followed.

Hopalong moved along, alert now. Then another rider joined the group from the north and one from the south, and he pushed on until all memory of time was lost and only the heat and the dust remained, the heat, the dust, and the trail of the horsemen.

Then from out of the distance came a long shout, then a shot. Suddenly there were other shots, and then toward him, from far off, came a horseman!

With incredible speed, he came on, heat waves making the image waver and shift. He was lashing a foam-flecked horse, riding as if the demons of hell were after him—and maybe they were!

Behind him pursued a dozen mounted men, their cloaks billowing out behind them. The rider saw Hopalong and swerved wide, racing toward a clump of brush and rocks; at the last moment his horse faltered. The riders cut across, and the lone man, who was Tredway, threw himself from his horse. He dodged and ran, stumbling in his haste, for the rocks.

He seemed to realize he was too slow, for he whirled and threw up his gun. The riders struck him then, and two of them grabbed his arms. His feet fought desperately to reach the earth, and from behind there was a volley of shots and the two riders dropped the lifeless body and charged on. Then they swung around and came back, and as they rode by each man fired a gun into the body of Tredway, and then, without seeming to notice Hopalong, they swung wide and rode off into the heat waves.

For a long time Hopalong sat on his horse, staring down at the crumpled, lifeless bundle of old clothes and used flesh that had been a man. When he looked up, it was to see Cindy Blair riding toward him; her clothes were torn and her cheek scratched.

"Are you all right?" he asked quickly.

She nodded, glancing at the dark bundle, then away. "They—the Brothers—they did that?"

He nodded. "Let's go home. Rig will be worried."

Almost an hour later she suddenly spoke. "They must have had their reasons."

"Yes."

"He told me about the PM. He transplanted a tree, grass, everything."

"I know. I figured it too late. Those stubbly limbs on that cottonwood, then the smaller ones growing out of them. I should have known it had been transplanted."

"Hoppy? He was Fan Harlan, wasn't he?"

"Sure. He never left this country for long. He was crazy to

come back, with the Brothers wanting him, but he saw his chance here, and he knew they never left their mesa."

They returned to the head of the canyon trail for Krug. The outlaw was gone. He had worked himself loose and escaped. "I'm not sorry," Hopalong told Cindy. "Maybe he's learned his lesson."

When they rode into the streets of Kachina, it was to find a crowd of horsemen all mounted to ride out after them. Rig explained they had been out searching, had lost the trail, and returned for fresh horses and food. Hopalong explained what had happened. As they talked Cindy suddenly caught Hoppy's arm. "Look!" she whispered. "Look at this!"

A dozen riders, clad in cloaks and hoods, rode down the streets in ranks of three. Before the saloon they stopped and one of them dismounted. He walked up to the wall and tacked a notice there. Mounting again, they turned and rode quietly out of town. Not until they were gone did anyone approach the notice.

Hopalong Cassidy leaned from his horse and read the words aloud.

"ATTENTION, CITIZENS OF KACHINA

"Be it known that the man calling himself Justin Tredway, known to the law as Fan Harlan, was an abandoned child adopted by the Brothers Penitentes;

"That upon leaving the Order, he stole the Treasury and he killed in cold blood two of the elders;

"That he brought disgrace upon us by his subsequent conduct; that he, by our records, robbed four trains, seventeen stages, killed eleven men and one woman;

"For this, in solemn conclave, the Brothers Penitentes have tried, judged, and sentenced to death the man John Woolrich, alias Fan Harlan, alias Justin Tredway.

"John Woolrich was executed at fifteen minutes past three o'clock this day."

Rig Taylor rode up beside Cindy and took her hand. Hopalong Cassidy turned away from the placard and swung his horse around. On the steps in front of the saloon a young man was sitting. He was neatly dressed, his gray shirt taut over a powerful chest, his naturally cold face now lighted by a smile.

"Mesquite Jenkins!" Hopalong exclaimed. "What are you doing here?"

"Well," he said, "I've got a loan for seven thousand dollars and I figured on starting a new ranch up Blue Mountain way. I was hopin' you'd help me out."

Over the mountains beyond Babylon Mesa heavy thunderheads had gathered. The heat still hung heavy in the sky, presaging the thunderstorm that was coming. Hopalong was tired, but once a job was done, he never could stay in one place for very long.

"All right." He turned to his friends. "It looks like I'm going to be heading out." Dismounting, he shook hands with Rig. Cindy Blair stepped up. "Thank you, Hoppy," she said, kissing him on the cheek. Sarah Towne took his hand and led him a few steps to where Pike was standing. "We're going to make a new life. In a few days we're going to head for Oregon."

"I'm glad," Hopalong told her. He shook hands with Pike; when Pike let go he grabbed Cassidy in a fierce bear hug that lifted Hopalong from the ground. The two men laughed.

"If you ever need me," the man who had once been Ben Hardy said, "I'll come a-runnin'."

Hopalong Cassidy swung into the saddle, and with Mesquite at his side the two started up the trail. In the distance a muffled avalanche of thunder rolled and rumbled. Through the storm clouds the afternoon sun sent streaks of cathedral light across the sky and the first spattering of drops fell, dappling the ground and making the dust jump.

"Red Connors is meeting me out there," Mesquite said as they rode out of town. "And if we can find Jonny, we'll send for him. It'll be like old times again."

"Well, lead on then," Hopalong Cassidy said, tugging his hat down on his head. "I always did like ridin' in the rain."

Pike Towne stood in the main street of Kachina long after the others had taken shelter inside the hotel. The warm rain tapped on his hat and slowly soaked through his shirt. He looked off across the country, watching the mounted figures of Hopalong Cassidy and Mesquite Jenkins as they followed the trail out of town, appearing and disappearing in the folds of the landscape, finally cresting a hill that would take them forever out of sight. The clouds had broken momentarily and the hill was drenched in golden shafts of light. One figure went on, but the other stopped on the crest of the hill and seemed to be looking back. Pike Towne thought he could see the figure lift a hand in farewell, but because of the distance, and the rain, he couldn't be sure.

A Final
Explanation, Thanks,
and Farewell

Here again is the brief version of my father's involvement with Hopalong Cassidy stories. For a more in-depth account please refer to the Afterword in *The Rustlers of West Fork*.

It goes like this . . . in the early 1950s, actor William Boyd took his version of the Cassidy character from the big screen to television. His earlier movies and Clarence Mulford's Hopalong books had been very popular and so Doubleday, Mulford's publisher, became interested in marketing some new Hoppy novels. Mulford, who had been retired since 1941, did not want to continue the job and so he turned the task over to a young (actually not that young; Dad was 42) writer of pulp magazine Westerns . . . Louis L'Amour.

The publishers chose the pen name Tex Burns for him and in 1950 and '51 he wrote his four Hopalong Cassidy books. They were published as the feature stories in *Hopalong Cassidy's Western Magazine*, and in hardcover by Doubleday. Due to a disagreement with the publisher over which interpretation of the

Hopalong character to use (Dad wanted to use Mulford's original Hoppy, a red-haired, hard-drinking, foul-mouthed, and rather bellicose cowhand instead of Doubleday's preference for the slick, heroic approach that Boyd adopted for his films), my father refused to admit that he had ever written those last four Hopalongs. Starting with *The Rustlers of West Fork*, this is the first time that they have ever been published with his name on them.

Trouble Shooter ended this period in Louis L'Amour's life; he went on to publish the novel *Hondo* under his own name in 1953. I have a report from a fan, Don Hant, that he discovered records in the Atlanta Public Library of a half-dozen or more Hopalong Cassidy stories written under the name Tex Burns. As far as I can tell only the four that Bantam has just published were actually written by Louis L'Amour. I assume that using the Tex Burns pseudonym the magazine went on to publish more issues with stories by another writer or writers.

I have also had some mail regarding an unresolved area of *The Riders of High Rock*. Several readers have written to me asking "What happened to Frank Gillespie?" The last we heard of him he had ridden off in pursuit of Jack Bolt, and Hopalong and his friends were following after. He's never heard from again. For both my father and myself there's only one thing I can say . . .

Sorry. We blew it.

So it's farewell to Hopalong, Tex Burns, and all the confusion. In the future you can look forward to several more books of short stories to be published at regular intervals and *The Louis L'Amour Western Magazine*, which should already be available as you read this. The magazine is our attempt to pass along some of the opportunities that my father found in the pulp magazines to new writers in the Western genre. I hope you'll like it.

I again offer my thanks to David R. Hastings II and Peter G. Hastings, Trustees of the Clarence E. Mulford Trust. Also to the late C. E. Mulford himself for creating the classic character of Hopalong Cassidy.

My best to you all,

BEAU L'AMOUR
Los Angeles, CA
September 1993

ABOUT LOUIS L'AMOUR

"I think of myself in the oral tradition—as a troubadour, a village tale-teller, the man in the shadows of the campfire. That's the way I'd like to be remembered—as a storyteller. A good storyteller."

It is doubtful that any author could be as at home in the world re-created in his novels as Louis Dearborn L'Amour. Not only could he physically fill the boots of the rugged characters he wrote about, but he literally "walked the land my characters walk." His personal experiences as well as his lifelong devotion to historical research combined to give Mr. L'Amour the unique knowledge and understanding of people, events, and the challenge of the American frontier that became the hallmarks of his popularity.

Of French-Irish descent, Mr. L'Amour could trace his own family in North America back to the early 1600s and follow their steady progression westward, "always on the frontier." As a boy growing up in Jamestown, North Dakota, he absorbed all he could about his family's frontier heritage, including the story of his great-grandfather who was scalped by Sioux warriors.

Spurred by an eager curiosity and desire to broaden his horizons, Mr. L'Amour left home at the age of fifteen and enjoyed a wide variety of jobs including seaman, lumberjack, elephant handler, skinner of dead cattle, assessment miner, and an officer in the tank destroyers during World War II. During his "yondering" days he also circled the world on a freighter, sailed a dhow on the Red Sea, was shipwrecked in the West Indies and stranded in the Mojave Desert. He won fifty-one of fifty-nine fights as a professional boxer and worked as a journalist and lecturer. He was a voracious reader and collector of rare books. His personal library contained 17,000 volumes.

Mr. L'Amour "wanted to write almost from the time I could talk." After developing a widespread following for his many frontier and adventure stories written for fiction magazines, Mr. L'Amour published his first full-length novel, *Hondo*, in the United States in 1953. Every one of his more than 100 books is in print; there are nearly 230 million copies of his books in print worldwide, making him one of the bestselling authors in modern literary history. His books have been translated into twenty languages, and more than forty-five of his novels and stories have been made into feature films and television movies.

His hardcover bestsellers include *The Lonesome Gods, The Walking Drum* (his twelfth-century historical novel), *Jubal Sackett, Last of the Breed,* and *The Haunted Mesa.* His memoir, *Education of a Wandering Man,* was a leading bestseller in 1989. Audio dramatizations and adaptations of many L'Amour stories are available on cassette tapes from Bantam Audio publishing.

The recipient of many great honors and awards, in 1983 Mr. L'Amour became the first novelist ever to be awarded the Congressional Gold Medal by the United States Congress in honor of his life's work. In 1984 he was also awarded the Medal of Freedom by President Reagan.

Louis L'Amour died on June 10, 1988. His wife, Kathy, and their two children, Beau and Angelique, carry the L'Amour tradition forward with new books written by the author during his lifetime to be published by Bantam well into the nineties.